11/96   Mobile

Mobile

SPECIAL MESSAGE TO READERS

I've travelled the world twice over,
Met the famous: saints and sinners,
Poets and artists, kings and queens,
Old stars and hopeful beginners,
I've been where no-one's been before,
Learned secrets from writers and cooks
All with one library ticket
To the wonderful world of books.

© JANICE JAMES.

THE FLYING GOAT

This is a collection of short stories from the author of THE DARLING BUDS OF MAY. In the title story the light-hearted comedy of his Uncle Silas sketches is given full play. In THE OX he handles the tragedy of a stoical, inexperienced woman. I AM NOT MYSELF, is a study of a man who falls in love with a girl who is not quite mad and yet who believes in the existence of things which do not exist. Its restrained atmosphere of tenderness and half-madness sets the story apart from all the rest.

H. E. BATES

◆

THE FLYING GOAT

Complete and Unabridged

ULVERSCROFT
Leicester

This edition first published
in Great Britain in 1993 by
Robert Hale Limited
London

First Large Print Edition
published December 1995
by arrangement with
Robert Hale Limited
London

British Library CIP Data

Bates, H. E.
The flying goat.—Large print ed.—
Ulverscroft large print series: general fiction
I. Title
823.912 [FS]

ISBN 0–7089–3423–4

Published by
F. A. Thorpe (Publishing) Ltd.
Anstey, Leicestershire

Set by Words & Graphics Ltd.
Anstey, Leicestershire
Printed and bound in Great Britain by
T. J. Press (Padstow) Ltd., Padstow, Cornwall

This book is printed on acid-free paper

To Richard Church

Contents

Contents

The White Pony

ALEXANDER went down the farm-yard past the hay stacks and the bramble cart-shed and out into the field beyond the sycamore trees, looking for the white pony. The mist of the summer morning lay cottoned far across the valley, so that he moved in a world above clouds that seemed to float upward and envelop him as he went down the slope. Here and there he came across places in the grass where the pony had lain during the night, buttercups and moon-daisies pressed flat as in a prayer-book by the fat flanks, and he could see where hoofs had broken the ground by stamping and had exploded the ginger ant-hills. But there was no white pony. The mist was creeping rapidly up the field and soon he could see nothing except grass and the floating foam of white and golden flowers flowing as on a smooth tide out of the mist, and could hear nothing except the blunted voices

1

of birds in the deep mist-silence of the fields.

The pony was a week old. Somewhere, for someone else, he had had another life, but for Alexander it had no meaning. All of his life that mattered had begun from the minute, a week past, when Uncle Bishop had bought him to replace the rough chestnut, and a new life had begun for Alexander. To the boy the white pony was now a miracle. "See how straight he stands," he had heard a man say. "Breedin' there. Mighta bin a race-horse." They called him Snowy, and he began to call the name as he went down the field, singing it, low and high, inverting the sound of the cuckoos coming from the spinneys. But there was still no pony and he went down to the farthest fences without seeing him. The pony had been there, kicking white scars into the ashpales sometime not long before, leaving fresh mushrooms of steaming dung in the grass. The boy stood swinging the halter like a lasso, wishing it could be a lasso and he himself a wild boy alone in a wild world.

After a minute he moved away, calling again, wondering a little, and at that instant the mist swung upwards. It seemed to lift with the suddenness of a released balloon, leaving the field suffused with warm apricot light, the daisies china-white in the sun, and in the centre of it the white pony standing dead still, feet together, head splendidly aloof and erect, a statue of chalk.

Seeing him, Alexander ran across the field, taking two haunches of bread out of his pocket as he went. The pony waited, not moving. "Snowy," the boy said, "Snowy." He held the bread out in one hand, flat, touching the pony's nose with the other, and the pony lowered his head and took the bread, the teeth warm and slimy on the palm of the boy's hand. After the bread had gone, Alexander fixed the halter. "Snowy," he kept saying, "Good boy, Snowy," deeply glad of the moment of being alone there with the horse, smelling the strong warm horse smell, feeling the sun already warm on his own neck and on the body of the horse as he led him away.

Back at the fence he drew the horse

closely parallel to the rails and then climbed up and got on. He sat well up, knees bent. The flanks of the pony under his bare knees seemed smoother and more friendly than anything on earth and as he moved forward the boy felt that he and the pony were part of each other, indivisible in a new affection. He moved gently and as the boy called him again "Snowy, giddup, Snowy," the ears flickered and were still in a second of response and knowledge. And suddenly, from the new height of the pony's back, the boy felt extraordinarily excited and solitary, completely alone in the side of the valley, with the sun breaking the mist and the fields lining up into distant battalions of colour and the farms waking beyond the river.

As he began to ride back to the farm the mood of pride and delight continued: his pony, his world, his time to use as he liked. He smoothed his hand down the pony's neck. The long muscles rippled like a strong current of water under his hand and he felt a sudden impulse to gallop. He took a quick look behind him and then let the pony go across the broad field, that was shut away from the farm-house by the spinneys. He dug his knees hard into the flanks and held the halter grimly with both hands and it seemed as if the response of the horse were electric. He's got racing blood all right, he thought. He's got it. He's a masterpiece, a wonder. The morning air was warm already as it rushed past his face and he saw the ground skidding dangerously away from him as the pony rose to the slope, his heart panting deeply as they reached the hurdle by the spinney, the beauty and exhilaration of speed exciting him down to the extreme tips of his limbs.

He dismounted at the hurdle and walked the rest of the way up to the house, past cart sheds and stacks and into the little rectangular farm-yard flanked by pig-sties and hen-houses. He led the horse with a kind of indifferent sedateness: the idea being innocence. "Don't you let that boy gallop that horse — you want to break his neck?" he remembered his Aunt Bishop's words, and then his Uncle Bishop's — "She says if you gallop him again she'll warm you

5

and pack you back home." But as he led the pony over to the stables there was no warning shout from anybody or anywhere. The yard was dead quiet, dung-steeped and drowsy already with sun, the pigs silent.

Suddenly, this deep silence seemed ominous.

He stopped by the stable door. Now, from the far side of the yard, from behind the hen-houses, he could hear voices. They seemed to be strange voices. They seemed to be arguing about something. Not understanding it, he listened for a moment and then tied the pony to the stable door and went across the yard.

"Th'aint bin a fox yit as could unscrew the side of a hen-place and walk out wi' the hens under his arm. So don't try and tell me they is."

"Oh! What's this then? Ain't they fox-marks? Just by your feet there? Plain as daylight."

"No, they ain't. Them are dug prints. I know dug prints when I see 'em."

"Yis, an' I know fox prints. I seen 'em afore."

"When?"

6

"Over at Jim Harris's place. When they lost that lot o' hens last Michaelmas. That was a fox all right, and so was this, I tell y'."

"Yis? I tell y' if this was a fox it was a two-legged 'un. Thass what it was."

Alexander stood by the corner of the hen-roost, listening, his mouth open. Three men were arguing: his Uncle Bishop, limbs as fat as bladders of lard in his shining trousers, a policeman in plain clothes, braces showing from under his open sports jacket, police boots gleaming from under police trousers, and Maxie, the cow-man, a cunning little man with small rivet eyes and a striped celluloid collar fixed with a brass stud and no tie.

It was Maxie who said: "Fox? If that was a fox I'm a bloody cart-horse. Ain't a fox as ever took twenty hens in one night."

"Only a two-legged fox," Uncle Bishop said.

"Oh, ain't they?" the policeman said.

"No, they ain't," Uncle Bishop said, "and I want summat done."

"Well," the policeman said, "jist as you

like, jist as you like. Have it your own
way. I'll git back to breakfast now and
be back in hour and do me measurin'
up. But if you be ruled by me you'll sit
up with a gun to-night."

* * *

An hour later that morning Alexander sat
on a wooden bin in the little hovel next
to the stable where corn was kept for the
hens and pollard for the pigs, and Maxie
sat on another bin, thumb on cold bacon
and bread, jack-knife upraised, having his
breakfast.

"Yis, boy," Maxie said, "it's a two-
legged fox or else my old woman's a
Dutchman, and she ain't. It's a two-
legged fox and we're goin' to git it.
To-night."

"How?"

"We're jis goin' wait," Maxie said, "jis
goin' wait wi' a coupla guns. Thass all.
And whoever it is'll git oles blown in 'is
trousis."

"Supposing he don't come to-night?"

"Then we're goin' wait till he does
come. We'll wait till bull's noon."

8

Maxie took a large piece of cold grey-red bacon on the end of his knife and with it a large piece of bread and put them both into his mouth. His little eyes bulged and stared like a hare's and something in his throat waggled up and down like an imprisoned frog. Alexander stared, fascinated, and said "You think you know who it is, Maxie?"

Maxie did not answer. He took up his beer-bottle, slowly unscrewed the stopper and wiped the top with his sleeve. He had the bland, secretive air of a man who has a miracle up his sleeve. His eyes, smaller now, were cocked at the distant dark cobwebs in the corners of the little hut. "I ain't sayin' I know. An' I ain't sayin' I don't know."

"But you've got an idea?"

Maxie tilted the bottle, closed his little weasel mouth over the top and the frog took a series of prolonged jumps in his throat. It was silent in the little hut while he drank, but outside the day was fully awake, the mist cleared away, the cuckoos in the spinney and down through the fields warmed into stuttering excitement of sun, the blackbirds rich and mad in the long hedge of pink-fading hawthorn dividing the road from the house. The boy felt a deep sense of excitement and secrecy in both sound and silence, and leaned forward to Maxie.

"I won't tell, Maxie. I'll keep it. I won't tell."

"Skin y-alive if you do."

"I won't tell."

"Well," Maxie said. He speared bread and bacon with his knife, held it aloft, and the boy waited in fascination and wonder. "No doubt about it," Maxie said. "Gippos."

"Does Uncle Bishop think it's gippos?"

"Yis," Maxie said. "Thinks like me. We know dug prints when we see 'em and we know fox-prints. And we know gippo prints."

"You think it's Shako?"

"Th' ain't no more gippos about here," Maxie said, "only Shako and his lot." He suddenly began to wave the knife at the boy, losing patience. "Y' Uncle Bishop's too easy, boy. Too easy. Lets 'em do what they like, don't he? Let's 'em have that field down by the brook don't he and don't charge nothing? Lets

10

'em leave a cart here when they move round and don't wanta to be bothered wi' too much clutter. Lets 'em come here cadgin'. Don't he? Mite o' straw, a few turnips, sack o' taters, anything. Don't he?"

"Yes."

"Well, you see where it gits 'im! Twenty hens gone in one night." Maxie got up, sharp snappy little voice like a terrier's, the back of his hand screwing crumbs and drink from his mouth. "But if I have my way it's gone far enough. I'll blow enough holes in Shako's behind to turn him into a bloody colander."

Maxie went out of the hut into the sunshine, the boy following him.

"You never see nothin' funny down in the field when you went to fetch Snowy, did you? No gates left open? No hen feathers about nowhere?"

"No. It was too misty to see."

"Well, you keep your eyes open. Very like you'll see summat yit."

Maxie moved over towards the stables. Alexander, fretted suddenly by wild ideas, inspired by Maxie's words, went with him. "You going to need Snowy this afternoon, Maxie?" he said.

"Well, I'm goin' to use him this morning to git a load or two o' faggots for a stack-bottom. Oughta be finished be dinner."

Maxie opened the lower half of the stable door. "Look a that," he said. The stable-pin had worked loose from its socket, the door was scarred by yellow slashes of hoofs. "Done that yesterday," Maxie said. "One day he'll kick the damn door down."

"He kicks that bottom fence like that. Kicks it to bits nearly every night."

"Yis, I know. Allus looks to me as if he's got too much energy. Wants to be kickin' and runnin' all the time."

"Do you think he was ever a race-horse?" Alexander said.

"Doubt it," Maxie said. "But he's good. He's got breedin'. Look at how he stan's. Look at it."

The boy looked lovingly at the horse. It was a joy to see him there, white and almost translucent in the darkness of the stable, the head motionless and well up, the black beautiful eyes alone moving under the tickling of a solitary fly. He

12

put one hand on the staunch smooth flank with a manly and important gesture of love and possession, and in that instant all the wild ideas in his mind crystallized into a proper purpose. He was so excited by that purpose that he hardly listened to Maxie saying something about "Well, it's no use, I gotta get harnessed up and doing something", his own words of departure so vague and sudden that he scarcely knew he had spoken them, "I'm going now, Maxie. Going to look for a pudden' bag's nest down the brook", Maxie's answer only reaching him after he was out in the sunshine again, "Bit late for a pudden-bag's, ain't it?" and even then not meaning anything.

He left the farm by the way he had come into it an hour or two before with the horse, going down by the stone track into the long field that sloped away to the brook and farther on to the river. It was hot now, the sky blue and silky, and he could see the heat dancing on the distances. As he went lower and lower down the slope, under the shelter of the big hawthorns and ashes and wind-beaten willows, the buttercups powdering his boots with a deep lemon dust of pollen, he felt himself sucked down by the luxuriance of summer into a world that seemed to belong to no one but himself. It gave a great sense of secrecy to what he was about to do. Farther down the slope the grasses were breast high and the path went through a narrow spinney of ash and poplar and flower-tousled elders on the fringe of it and a floor of dead bluebells, bringing him out at the other side on the crest of short stone cliff, once a quarry face, with a grass road and the brook itself flowing along in the hollow underneath.

He went cautiously out of the spinney and, behind a large hawthorn that had already shed its flowers like drifts of washed pink and orange confetti, lay down on his belly. He could see, on the old grass road directly below, the gipsy camp: the round yellow varnished caravan, a couple of disused prams, washing spread on the grass, a black mare hobbled and grazing on the brook edge, a fire slowly eating a grey white hole in the bright grass. He took it in without any great excitement, as something he had seen before. What excited him were the things he couldn't see.

The trap wasn't there, and the strong brown little cob that went with it. The women weren't there. More important still, there was no sign of Shako and the men. There was no sign of life except the mare and the washing on the grass. Although he lay with his heart pumping madly into the grass, it was all as he had expected it, as he hoped it would be. He took the signs of suspicion and fused them by the heat of momentary excitement into a conviction of Shako's guilt.

He waited for a long time, the sun hot on his back and the back of his neck, for something to happen. But almost nothing moved in the hollow below him except the mare taking limping steps along the brook-side, working her way into a shade, and a solitary kingfisher swooping up the brook and then sometime afterwards down again, a blue electric message sparking in and out of the overhanging leaves.

It was almost half an hour later when he slipped quietly down the short grass

15

of the slope between the stunted bushes of seedling hawthorn and the ledges of overhanging rock, warm as new eggs on the palm of his hand as he rested his weight on them. He went cautiously and, though his whole body was beating excitement, with that air of indifferent innocence he had used back in the farmyard. Down in the camp he saw that the fire, almost out now, must have been lighted hours before. He put his hand on an iron-grey shirt of Shakos lying on the ground in the sun. It was so dry that it seemed to lie stiffly perched on the tops of the buttercup stems. Then he saw something else. It startled him so much that he felt his head rock faintly in the sun.

On the grass, among many new prints of horses hoofs, lay odd lumps of grey-green hen dung. He turned one over with his dust-yellow boots. It was fresh and soft. Then suddenly he thought of something else: feathers. He began to walk about, his eyes searching the grass, his excitement and the heat in the sheltered hollow making him almost sick. He had hardly moved a dozen yards when he heard a shout. "Hi! Hi'yup!" It came from the far bank of the brook and it came with a shrill unexpectedness that made his heart go off like a trap.

He stood very still, scared, waiting. He saw the elder branches on the bank of the brook stir and shake apart. He felt a second of intense fear, then another of intense relief.

Coming up from the brook was young Shako: the boy of his own age, in man's cap and long trousers braced up with binder string, eyes deep and bright as blackberries in the sun, coal-coloured hair hanging in bobtail curls in his neck.

"Hi! What you doin'?" He had a flat osier basket of watercresses in his hand.

"Looking for you," Alexander said. "Thought there was nobody here."

"Lookin' for me?"

Alexander's fear seemed to evaporate through his mouth, leaving his tongue queer and dry. He and young Shako knew each other. Young Shako had often been up at the farm; once they had tried fishing for young silver trout no bigger than teaspoons in the upper reaches of

17

the stream. Shako had seen Snowy too.

"Yes," Alexander said. "When're you coming for a ride with the cob and me and Snowy? You reckoned you'd come this week."

"Won't be to-day," young Shako said. "The cob ain' here."

"Where's he gone?" Alexander said. "Where's everybody?"

"Old Gal's hawkin' down in Ferrers. Dad and Charley and Plum gone over to Huntingdon."

"Long way."

"Ain't nothing," young Shako said. "Jis skipped over about some ducks."

"Ducks?"

"Selling some ducks or summat."

Young Shako sat down on the grass, Alexander with him, careless, as though he knew nothing and nothing had happened. Ducks? Ducks was funny. He lay on the grass, some inner part of himself alert and listening. Ducks was very funny.

"You said we'd have a race," he said. "You on the cob and me on Snowy."

"Cob'd eat 'im."

"Who would? What would?" Alexander

18

said. "Snowy's been a race-horse."

"Well, so's the cob. We bought 'im from a jockey fella. Out at Newmarket. Jockey fella named Adams. Best jockey in England. You heard on 'im ain' y?"

"Yes, but what's that? Snowy's a real race-horse. You can see it. Some hunters came by the other day and he nearly went mad. He can smell the difference in horses. Besides, we know he's been a race-horse. Ask Maxie. He's got his pedigree."

"Pedigree? What the blarming oojah?" Young Shako said. "That's nothing. You know what a pedigree is?"

"Yes."

"What is it?"

"Well, it's what he is. What he's been."

"What the blarming oojah?" Shako said. "It's summat wrong with 'is legs. Any fool knows that. Pedigree — any fool knows it's summat wrong wi' his legs."

Alexander sat silent, almost defeated, then coming back again.

"You're frightened to race, that's all. Make out the cob's gone to Huntingdon because you daren't race."

"Frit?" Shako said. "Who's frit? I'll race y' any day. Any time."

"All right. To-morrow," Alexander said.

"No."

"See. I told you. Daren't."

"What the blarming oojah! They ain't goin' be back from Huntingdon till Friday."

Alexander stared at the sky, indifferent.

"What time did they go?" he said.

"Middle o' the night sometime," young Shako said. "They were gone when I got up."

They lay for a little while longer on the grass, talking, young Shako trying to talk of big two-pound trout seen farther downstream, in the still golden hollows of the backwater where the mill had been, but the mind of Alexander could not concentrate and he had eyes for nothing except the tiniest of sand-coloured hen feathers clinging like extra petals to the edges of flowers and grass, suddenly visible because he could see them horizontally, a hen's-eye view — the same pale creamy-brown feathers that he sometimes found stuck by blood to the eggs that he collected morning and evening from the orange-boxes in the hen-roost at the farm. When he saw them, realizing fully what they meant, he lost track of what Shako was saying altogether. He got to his feet and made some excuse about going back to the farm. Shako got to his feet too, saying, "Yis, I gotta meet the old woman and hawk this cress", his deep black eyes careless and tired and Spaniard-like in the full sun, his voice calling Alexander back from the dozen paces he had taken across the field.

"You wanna race Friday I'll race you if they're back. If they ain't back I'll race you Saturday."

"All right." In that second Alexander came to his senses. "I'll come down and see when they are back," he said.

He made the climb back up the slope, over the warm projecting rocks and up through the spinney and into the warm security of the breast-high grasses beyond it in a state of such excitement that he could not think or speak to himself. He could only beat his hands like drumsticks on his brown bare knees in a tattoo of triumph and delight.

* * *

That night he knew that his uncle Bishop and Maxie sat up in the farm-yard with loaded guns, Maxie in the little corn-hovel, his Uncle under the cart-shed, from somewhere about midnight to the first colour of daylight about three o'clock, waiting for Shako. In the small back bedroom where in autumn and winter the long brown-papered trays of apples and pears would be laid out under his bed and over every inch of the cold linoleum of the floor, so that there was a good excuse for never kneeling to say his prayers, he kept awake for a long time, listening for something to happen, yet hoping and really knowing it wouldn't happen, suddenly falling asleep in a moment when as it were he wasn't looking, and waking an hour too late to fetch Snowy from the field.

Of what had happened down at the brook with young Shako he did not say a word all that day, Thursday, and all the next. He heard more talk of two-legged foxes, talked to Maxie himself of the way the men had sat up listening and waiting and hearing nothing but the sound of Snowy kicking the fences over the dead quiet fields. He saw the constable come into the yard again, making a pretence of taking measurements, arguing, really whiling away, as Maxie said, the bleedin' government's time and doing nothing. He knew that his Uncle and Maxie sat up that night again, waiting for a Shako that he alone knew would not come, and he let it happen partly out of a queer impulse of secrecy and partly because of a fear that no one would ever believe his simple and exciting piece of detective fantasy.

It was Friday afternoon when he rode Snowy down the track by the spinney and out across the buttercup field and down to the edge of the quarry. He sat bare-back, the only way he knew how to ride, and the warm sweat of a canter in the hot sun across the shadeless field broke out on his legs and seemed to glue him to the pony. The delight of being alone, in the heat and silence of a midsummer afternoon that seemed to grow more and more intense as the ripe grasses deepened about the pony's legs like dusty wheat, was something he loved and could hardly bear. The may-blossom was over now, like cream soured and gone in the sun, and elderberry had taken its place, sweet-sour itself, the summery vanilla odour putting the whole sheltered hollow to sleep. So that as he halted Snowy and called down to the camp to young Shako, who was lying alone in the grass by the side of the hobbled little brown cob, his voice was like the sudden cracking of a cup in the stillness.

"Ready to race?"

"Eh?"

Young Shako turned sharply and rolled to his feet like a black untidy puppy, blinking in the sun.

"Now?" he called back.

"It's Friday!" Alexander said. "You said Friday."

"Right-o! Wait'll I git the cob."

Young Shako began to untie the rope hobbling the cob's fore-legs, but Alexander was no longer looking at him. The camp was deserted again except for the cob and the boy, but down under the caravan Alexander could see suddenly a white-washed crate, an empty hen-crate. It startled and excited him so much that he hardly realized that Young Shako was ready and already calling his name.

"Hiyup! You go along the top and I'll go along the bottom and meet you!"

"Right-o!"

Alexander turned the white pony and almost simultaneously young Shako scrambled belly-wise on the cob's back and turned him in the same direction along the brookside. They rode along together, hoofs making no noise in the thick grass, the excitement of silence beating deeply in the boy's breast and throat. It seemed to him too that Snowy was excited, sensing something. His head seemed exceptionally high up, splendid in the sun, with a sort of alert nobility, his beauty and strength flowing out to the boy, so that he felt outlandishly proud and strong himself.

Gradually the quarry-face shallowed down until the land was entirely on one level. Alexander halted Snowy and waited for young Shako to come up to him. The land had begun to be broken up by sedge and to Alexander it looked as though the cob, struggling between the stiff rushes on ground bubbled by ant-hills, was ugly and ordinary and short-winded. Until that moment the boys had not spoken again, but now Shako said where were they going to race? Up on the top field above the marsh? And Alexander said "Yes, up in the top field," and they rode the horses away from the brook together, skirting the marsh where even the high spears of reed were dead still in the windless afternoon, blades of dark green steel sharp in the sun above the torches of lemon iris and islands of emerald grass among the fly-freckled pools.

"So they got back from Huntingdon?" Alexander said.

"Yeh! Got back. Got back late last night."

"Gone somewhere to-day?"

"Only down to the market. Be back any time now."

"How far are we going to race?"

"Far as you like."

"Make it from the fence over to the first sycamore, shall we?" Alexander said.

"Ain't very far."

"All right. Make it from the fence over to the feed-trough. That's a good way."

"All right," Shako said. "Anybody who falls off loses."

The sun beat down on them strongly as they turned up the field to meet it. Snowy lifted his head and Alexander could feel in him a sudden excited vibration of strength. His own heart was beating with such deep sickness that as they reached the fences and turned the horses he could not speak. He sat tense and silent, his senses cancelled out by the suspense of excitement. In this moment the world too was cancelled out except for the dazzling blaze of buttercups and the poised chalk statue of Snowy's head and the murmur of grasshoppers breaking and carrying away the silence on tremulous and infinite waves of sound.

Another second and young Shako counted three and lifted his hand and dropped it and Alexander did not know anything except that something amazing and unearthly happened to Snowy. He became something tearing its way off the golden rim of the earth. He felt him to be like a great white hare bouncing madly into space. He leaned forward and clung to his neck, frightened of falling or being thrown. The sycamore trees sailed past like balloons broken adrift and five seconds later he saw the two stone feed-troughs flash past him like boats torn from their moorings too.

Snowy did not come to a standstill until they reached the hedge and the end of the field. He stood for a moment fretting and panting deeply. It had been like a burst of majestic fury. It filled Alexander with a pride and astonishment that momentarily took his speech away, so that as he turned and saw young Shako and the cob clumsily pulling up at the troughs he could not speak.

He walked Snowy slowly back. His pride was one with the pony's, deep, quiet, almost dignified. It sprang out of the pony's heart. It stirred him to a few seconds of such love for the horse that he suddenly dismounted and seized his warm dribbling head in his hands.

"You see, I told you," he said to Shako at last. "He's been a race-horse."

"Wadn't much," Shako said. The deep Spaniard eyes were prouder in defeat than Alexander's were in triumph. "Cob was just tired after that long journey from Huntingdon. Bet y' I'd race you to-morrow and win y' easy. What y' goin' be up to now? Going home?"

Alexander remembered how Old Shako and his brothers Plum and Charley must be back from market soon, perhaps now, already.

"No," he said, "I'll come back a bit with you. Cool Snowy off and perhaps give him a drink."

"Don't wanna give him no drink while he's so ragin' hot."

"No, I know that. I'll just walk steady back with you. I want a drink myself."

They walked back down the field towards the stream, not saying much. Snowy was oily with sweat and the heat caught Alexander in the nape of the neck like a blow as they came into the sheltered ground beyond the quarry.

It was at that moment he saw that old Shako and Plum and Charley were back, one of the women with them. He saw the flare of the woman's yellow blouse and the dark beet-red skirt. The men were gaunt, hungry as hawks, shifty, with untranslatable darkness behind the friendliness of their eyes.

"Young Bish!" Old Shako said. He grinned with white eager teeth. "Thass nice pony you got. Fus' time I see him."

"Nice pony," Shako's brothers said.

The three men came round the horse, laying long dark hands on the white flanks.

"Nice pony." Old Shako looked at Snowy's mouth, and Alexander felt proud that Snowy stood so still and lovably dignified.

"Nice pony. On'y thing is he's gettin' old," Shako said. "Been about awhile."

"Nice pony though," Charley said.

"Yis. Nice pony," Shako said. "You wanna look after him. Be gettin' 'im pinched else. Nice pony like that."

The dark hands were smoothed on the white flanks again, and it seemed suddenly to Alexander that they might be hands of possession. His fears were suddenly heightened by something Shako said. "Knew a man once, Cakey Smith, he had a white horse and got it pinched. Somebody painted it black. Right, ain't it, Charley?"

"Right," Charley said.

Alexander did not speak. He knew that they were kidding him. He saw sparks of lying winks flash out of Shako's eyes, but he was suddenly frightened. He got hold of Snowy's bridle and prepared to lead him away and all at once the woman's voice came sing-songing from the caravan:

"Oh! the boy's lucky. Got a lucky face all right. Got a lucky face. Nobody'll pinch nothing from him. A lucky nice face he's got. Lucky. He'll be all right."

"Well, so long," Alexander said.

"So long," young Shako said. "Race y' to-morrow if y' want."

Suddenly Alexander's wits came back. He remembered why he was here, what it was all about. He remembered what his wild plan had been.

"I can't come to-morrow," he said. "Not Saturday." He felt new sweat break and flush his face as he told the lie. "We're going out. All of us. Over to

31

Aunt Tilda's for the night. Going to-morrow afternoon and not coming back till Sunday."

"Lucky boy," the woman said. "Oh! You're a lucky boy."

He walked away with her voice following him calling him lucky, and feeling the sombre eyes of the men swivelling after him. Once up the slope and beyond the spinney he could not walk fast enough. He stopped Snowy by a fence and got on his back. He rode up the track under a deep impulse of excitement and an imagination flared by the behaviour of Snowy and the gipsies and all he had heard.

He rode into the farmyard to put up the basking hens in a scared squawking clutter of brown and white wings. He leapt off the horse and felt the terrific excitement of a kind of heroism as he ran into the house, knowing that the time had come when he could keep things to himself no longer, knowing that he had to tell somebody now.

★ ★ ★

The following night, Saturday, Alexander lay in the little iron bedstead in the apple bedroom with his trousers on and his boots in readiness under the bed. "No!" Aunt Bishop had said, "they ain't goin' to sit up for no fox and no nothing else, so there! And even if they was you'd get to bed and get your sleep just the same. So don't whittle your belly about that!"

Very excited, he lay listening for a long time in the warm darkness of the little room. Twice he got up and stood at the window and looked out, smelling the summer night, seeing nothing to break the colour of darkness except the rosy-orange flowering of distant iron-ore furnaces on the hills beyond the river, hearing nothing to break the sound except a momentary lift of breeze stirring the pear-leaves on the house-wall under the window. For long periods he sat up in bed, eyes wide open so that they should not close altogether, and once he got up and, for the first time in his life, voluntarily washed his face. The cold water woke him afresh and after what seemed to him hours he heard the twang-clanging of the American clock, with the view of Philadelphia 1867, being wound by his Aunt Bishop in the living-room below, and then her feet on the stairs and finally the latch of her bed-room door breaking one silence and beginning another.

He waited for what he felt was five minutes and then got up and put on his jacket and tied his boots round his neck. He opened the door of his room and waited, listening. His heart seemed to pound at the darkness. He knew that the stairs creaked at every step and finally he lay on the banisters and slid down with no sound but a faint snake-like slither. The kitchen door was unlocked and he went out that way, sitting on the doormat to put on his boots.

In the darkness his senses were so sharpened by excitement that he could feel the presence of his Uncle Bishop and Maxie before he heard the whispers of their voices. They were sitting together under the cart-shed. For a minute he did not know what to do. Then he remembered the warm kindly face of his Uncle Bishop and the favourite phrase of his aunt, "Can't see nothing wrong in that boy, can you? I don' know! You'd give him your head if he asked for it," and he ran suddenly across the stack-yard, calling in a whisper who he was. "It's all right, it's me, it's Alexander", his heart bumping with guilt and excitement.

"Be God, you'll git me hung," his Uncle Bishop said.

"Lucky for you y'aint in Kingdom Come," Maxie said. "I was half a mind to shoot."

"Young gallus!" his uncle said. "Frightning folks to death."

"Can I stop?" Alexander said.

"Looks as y're stopping," Maxie said. "Jis be quiet. Y' oughta ding 'is ear," he said to Uncle Bishop. "Too soft with 'im be 'arf."

"I told you they were coming," Alexander said.

"We don' know as they are coming," Maxie said, "yit."

For a long time nobody spoke again. The fields were dead silent all round the house and when Alexander looked out from the hovel he was so excited that he felt that the stars swung in their courses over the straw-stacks and the trees. His hands trembled and he pressed them between his knees to quieten them. And then he heard something. It startled him by its closeness and familiarity: the clopping of Snowy's hoofs on the ground.

"Where's Snowy?" he said.

"In the stable," Maxie said. "We shut him up so's they should think we'd really gone. See?"

"Diddling 'em?"

"Diddlin' 'em," Maxie said. "Gotta be artful wi' gippos. Else they diddle you."

They sat silent for a long time again, the night broken by no sound except the occasional clop of Snowy's hoofs and a brief whisking of wind stirring into the stacks and sometimes an odd sleepy murmur from the hens. A sort of drugged suspense took hold of Alexander, so that once he lost count of time and place and himself, as though he were asleep on his feet.

It was Maxie's voice that sprung him back to full consciousness and excitement. "Ain't that somebody moochin' about behind the pig-sties?"

"Somebody or summat round there. Them 'ugs ain't rootlin' up for nothing."

"Listen! Somebody's comin' up round the back."

Alexander and the two men sat tense, waiting. The boy could hear the sound of someone moving in the deep nettles and grass behind the pig-sties. The sound came nearer, was in the yard itself, was translated suddenly into moving figures. Maxie moved out of the hovel. The boy knelt on his hands and knees, clawing with his finger nails at a flint embedded in the dry earth, loosening it at last and weighing it in his hand. He felt astonishingly brave and angry and excited. Down across the yard there was a sound of wood being gently splintered: of the plank, as before, being prised out of the side of the locked hen-house. As he heard it he felt the pressure of his Uncle Bishop's hand against his chest, forcing him back a pace or two into the cart-shed. As he moved back he caught his heel against the lowered shaft of the pony cart and slipped. He groped wildly and fell against the side of the shed, the impact clattering the loose corrugated iron roof like a tin skeleton.

When he picked himself up again Maxie and his uncle were already running across the yard, shouting. He began running too. Somebody was slashing a way out through the nettles behind the pig-sties, out towards the orchard. The sows had woken up and were thundering against the sty-doors and the hens had set up a wild cluttering of terror. Alexander flung the flint wildly in the darkness. It hit the iron roof of the pig-sties like a huge explosive cap going off and the next moment, at the gate of the orchard, Maxie fired a shot. For a moment Alexander felt that he had been knocked off his feet. The shot seemed to reverberate across half the world, the boomerang of echoes came smashing back and stirred cattle and hens and pigs to hysteria in which he too was yelling madly.

He was half way across the orchard, Maxie in front, his Uncle Bishop waddling behind, the gippos already lost somewhere beyond the farthest trees, when he realized that there was a new sound of hysteria in the yard behind him. He stopped, and knew suddenly that it was Snowy, kicking the stable down.

He ran straight back, seeing better now in the darkness but still blundering against low branches of fruit-trees, barking his shins on pig-troughs in the stack-yard, brushing past the fat outspread arms of his Uncle Bishop, yelling at him to come. As he reached the stack-yard, mounting straight over the muck-hill, he heard the crack of the stable-door as it split the staple and the final frenzied hammering of Snowy's hoofs as they beat back the swinging door again and again until Snowy himself was free. The horse swung out of the dark hole of the stable like the ghost of a flying horse on a roundabout, circling wildly out of sight behind the far stacks, making drivelling noises of terror. The boy ran to and fro in the dark yard like someone demented himself, calling his uncle, then Maxie.

"Be God, what the nation is it? Boy, what is it? Boy, wheer the devil are y'?"

"It's Snowy!" he yelled. "Maxie! It's Snowy. It's Snowy. Maxie! Uncle!"

He was almost crying now. The men

were rushing about the yard. His Aunt Bishop, from an upstairs window, was shouting incomprehensible threats or questions or advice, no one listening to her.

They were listening only to Alexander, to what he had to say. "Which way did he go, boy? Did you see him go? Which way?" And when he had nothing to say except "I saw him go by the stacks, that's all," they stood listening to a sound coming from far down the road, and he stood listening with them, his heart very scared, fear and excitement beating his brain dizzy.

It was a sound like the noise of a tune played on handbones: the sound of Snowy galloping on the road, far away already towards the river.

* * *

By nine o'clock on Sunday morning the three of them, Uncle Bishop and Maxie with Alexander riding on the carrier of Maxie's bicycle, had reached a point where the brook ran over the road, under a white hand-rail bridge between an

40

arch of alders, four miles upstream. Zig-zagging across the countryside, they had been riding and walking since six o'clock, asking everyone they met, a shepherd with his dog, a parson out walking before breakfast, labourers, a tramp or two: "Y' ain't seen a white horse nowhere? Got out last night. Ain't got no bridle on nor nothing," but no one had seen him and Alexander's heart had begun to curl up like a small tired animal on the verge of sickness.

A small hill, not much more than a green breastwork, curved up from one side of the brook, and Maxie clambered up it on thick squat legs to take a squint over the surrounding land. He came down shaking his head, pressing tired heels in the slope. Sun hit the bubbling surface of the water as it lippled over the road, the dazzling quicksilver light flashing back in Alexander's eyes, making him tired too.

"No sign on 'im," Maxie said. "No tellin' wheer he is got to. Rate he was runnin' he'll very like be half-way round England."

"More likely busted isself up on

something. On a fence or something, barbed wire or something," Uncle Bishop said.

"Well," Maxie said, "ain't no use stannin' about. Let's get on as far as Shelton. We can ask Fat Sturman if he's seed 'im."

"Fat Sturman?" Uncle Bishop said. "It's Sunday morning. He won't be able to tell a white horse from a black for another twenty-four hours. Allus sozzled Saddays and Sundays, you know that."

"I forgot," Maxie said. "Well, we can ask somebody. Ask the fust man we meet."

They walked despondently up the hill, pushing the bicycles. It was hot and silent everywhere, bees thick in the grass, the flat empty Sunday morning stillness seeming to Alexander to stretch far over the quivering horizon. Climbing, he looked at his boots. The lace-holes looked back at him from the pollen-yellow leather with the sad stoical eyes of Chinamen.

When he looked up again he was surprised to see an oldish woman coming down the hill, walking in a prim lardidardy way as though she had springs in the heels of her flat cloth-sided boots. On the top of an ant-hill of grey hair she had a huge fruit basket of a hat that reminded him of the glass-case of artificial grapes and pears and cherries that stood on the bible in his Aunt Bishop's parlour. The woman was carrying a prayer-book in her hands and Alexander could see her turning to smile at the trees as she went past, as though she had hidden friends in them.

"Shall we ask her?" Uncle Bishop whispered.

"Won't know a horse from a dead donkey," Maxie said.

"Never know," Uncle Bishop said. "Way she's bouncing down the hill she might a bin a jockey."

"Well, you ask her. Not me."

Half a minute later Uncle Bishop had taken off his hat and was making a little speech in a strange aristocratic voice to the old lady, who stood with hands clasped over the prayer-book, smiling with a kind of saintly beatitude. "Hexcuse me, madam, but hi suppose you hain't seen a white pony nowheer? Hescaped last night. Much hobliged lady, if you seen hany sign on 'im."

The old lady took one smiling, saintly look at the two men and Alexander.

"Yes," she said, "I have."

"My God," Maxie said, "wheer?"

The old lady looked at Maxie. "Did you use the name of God?"

"Yis, but — "

"In front of the little boy?"

"Yis, but — "

"My man, you ought to burn in hell!"

Sheepish and exasperated and at a loss, Uncle Bishop and Maxie stood looking at the ground, not knowing what to say, and the old lady suddenly began to make a strange rambling speech of reproval, preaching decency and godliness and respect for the Sabbath, her voice by turns like vinegar and honey, one hand sometimes upraised in a little gesture to the sky, until finally Alexander could stand it no longer.

"Please," he said, "please tell us where the horse is. Something might have happened to him. He might be bad. He might be dying."

"Everybody is dying," she said.

His heart sank; tears of anger and frustration hit his eyes and sprang back. "Tell us where he is," he said. "Please. Tell us where he is."

She was still smiling, saintly, slightly but rather nicely mad, and for one second the boy did not believe a word of all she had said. Then all at once she turned and pointed up the hill.

"He's at the top of the hill. Lying on the grass. Lying under a tree."

Maxie and Alexander and Uncle Bishop ran up the hill. "God bless you," the old lady called, but they scarcely heard it.

The white pony was lying as the old lady had said in the shade of an ash tree at the top of the hill. As he heard footsteps and voices he lifted his head, and a small black explosion of flies rose from one eye. The boy called his name and with a great eager effort, making odd noises in his throat, the pony tried to struggle to his feet. He made the effort and sank back and Maxie knelt down by his head. "All right, Snowy. All right. Goo' boy. Goo' boy then. All right."

"We got to git 'im up," Uncle Bishop said.

"Yis," Maxie said, "we got to git 'im up. Stan' back, boy. Very like he'll make a bit of a to-do. Stan' back."

Alexander stood back but the white pony could not rise. "Come on Snowy," the men said, "come on now. Come on," but nothing happened. It was cool under the ash tree but it seemed to the boy that the pony was held down by the heat of a great exhaustion. Each time he lifted his head the flies broke away in a small black explosion and then settled again.

They tried for almost half an hour to get the pony to his feet, but Maxie said at last: "It's no good. We gotta git somebody else to look at him. You wait here and I'll bike into Shelton and git Jeff Emery. He's a knacker."

"Knacker?" Uncle Bishop said.

"Well, he's a bit of a vet too. Does both. He'll know what to do if anybody does."

Maxie got on his bicycle and rode away up the hill. Alexander and Uncle Bishop stood and looked at the white pony. The depth of silence seemed to increase when Maxie had gone, bees moaning in the honeysuckle and the blackberry flowers,

46

yellow hammers chipping mournful notes on the hedgerows, a bell for morning service donging a thin hole in the distance over the hill.

"Think he'll get up?" the boy said.

"He'll get up, he's just tired. You would be if you'd galloped about all night."

"Shako says he's old. He's not, is he?"

"He ain't young."

"You think he's been a race-horse and the shot made him think he was in a race again?"

"I count that's what it was." Uncle Bishop took another look at the pony. "Well, it's no good. I gotta see a man about a dog. You comin'?" and he and Alexander went and stood over by the far hedge. "Hedge-roses out nice," Uncle Bishop said. "Grow all the better for a little water."

When they turned again something had happened. Very quiet and looking in some way very fragile, the white pony was on his feet. The boy's heart seemed to turn somersaults of happiness. He ran and put his hands on the pony's head, smoothing his nose, talking softly. "Snowy. Good Snowy. Good boy, Snowy."

"You think he's all right?" he said.

"You think he could walk as far as the brook? Perhaps he wants a drink?"

"Yeh. Let him walk if he will. Don't force him. Let him go how he likes."

"Come on, Snowy," the boy said. "Come on, Snowy. Good Snowy. Good boy. Come on."

The pony walked slowly down the hill in hot sunshine. At the bottom of the hill, where the brook ran over the road, he put his lips to the water. He let the water run into and past his mouth, not really drinking. He stood like that for a long time, not moving at all.

Suddenly he went down on his forelegs and sank into the water. Alexander and Uncle Bishop had not time to do anything before they heard a shout and saw Maxie, with a man in breeches and leggings, coming down the hill.

"Summat we can do, Jeff, ain't there?" Maxie said. "Summat we can do?"

The man did not answer. He knelt down by the pony, pressing his hands gently on the flanks.

"Well, there's jis' one thing we can do, that's all."

The boy stood scared and dumb, watching the water break against the body of the horse, not seeing the men's faces.

"All right," Maxie said. He took Alexander by the arm. "Boy, you git hold o' my bike and take it across the bridge and put it underneath that furdest ash tree, outa the sun. I don't want the tyres bustin'."

"Is Snowy going to be all right?" the boy said.

"Yis. He's going to be all right."

Alexander took the bicycle and wheeled it across the bridge and along the road. The ash tree was fifty yards away. He reached it and laid the bicycle against the trunk in the shade. The bell tinkled as it touched the tree and at the same time as if the bell were a signal, he heard a sharp, dull report from the brook, and he turned in time to see the man in breeches and leggings holding a strange-looking pistol in his hand.

Running wildly back to the brook, trying to shout and not shouting, he saw the white pony's head lying flat and limp in the water. The water was lapping over the eyes, and out of the head and mouth a long scarf of blood was slowly unwinding itself downstream. The men had their backs turned away from him as though they did not want to look at him, and he knew that the white pony had gone for ever.

What he did not know until long afterwards was that there, at that moment, in the dead silence of the summer morning, with the sun blazing down on the white pony and the crimson water and the buttercups rich as paint in the grass, some part of his life had gone for ever too.

Every Bullet Has Its Billet

IRMA HARRIS was eighteen when, in 1915, Lieutenant Bronson and his wife came to be billeted on her mother. Just out of High School, a pale arch-eyed girl with great masses of reddish gold hair scrolled up behind like the twists of a golden loaf, she had got to the age when she liked sitting for long hours in her own room, alone, thinking inexpressibly sad thoughts, with her hands spread out on her lap like two pink self-conscious flowers, waiting for the dew of all sorts of confused dreams to fall on them. Lieutenant Bronson and his wife had been married six weeks, and were very happy.

Mrs. Harris was a woman whose mind was done up in curling-rags: a plain, common mind which, for forty years, she had tried to frill into superiority. On a level above the neighbours, to whom she never spoke, she thanked God for Irma: thanked God that Irma's hair

51

was rich and beautiful, that she had the aristocratic richness of a name like Irma and not the common poverty of a name like May or Flo, that Irma had been educated, was superior, had kept pure and would, by the Grace of God, still keep pure for a long time to come. Earlier, some years before the death of Harris, who had peddled hosiery on a basket bicycle from door to door and had somehow cheese-pared his way to saving money, she had shut Irma down under a glass case, and had then gone on polishing the glass until she could see in it not only Irma but her own face. Even then it was not her own plain, ordinary curl-ragged face, but a face with a great mass of loaf-gold hair and soft pure skin as pale as bread. She saw Irma: Irma was herself. The girl was the lost self of the woman, unrecapturable except through the glass dome of imagination. Whatever might happen to Irma would happen also to herself.

In a podgy kind of way, Lieutenant Bronson was handsome, heavily built, with aristocratically tender feet which suffered terribly on the route marches. He came from the real aristocracy: estates in Cornwall, a house in Grosvenor Square, and at the outbreak of the war had been toying away time, on a pretence of working at oil, in Mexico. Yet he had a quality of self-effacement about him, a retreating charm of manner that was quite humble. The men liked him. He had a way of hushing up, as it were, his aristocratic identity. His wife was a little thing, a woman of whipped cream, delicate and sweet, all pretty froth and hardly tangible. An aristocrat also, she had not quite come to her senses after the tremendous crash of war and marriage coming almost at the same time, and she painted water-colours in the Harris's front room, in the real pre-war aristocratic mode, still nursing the idea that painting was a necessary accomplishment. Bronson adored her, and she was only bored when route-marches and parades and mess-duty claimed him too long. Then she painted hard, or wrote letters, or, on desperate days, went into the kitchen and prepared the anchovies or mayonnaise. On still more desperate days she invited Irma into the front room, to talk to her, while she painted.

The two girls liked each other. Only the thinnest veil of breeding and self-consciousness kept them apart, sometimes miles apart. Virginal, under the glass-case, Irma looked up to the older girl, envying the strange state of marriage, in which freedom and stability were so miraculously combined. Whirling round on an axis which marriage and war had sent crazy, Mrs. Bronson looked down, with slight envy, on what she felt to be Irma's state of emotional rest.

Mrs. Bronson painted with timid accurate talent, creating nothing. The delicate water-colours cost her no emotion. She copied flowers, did a bowl of Gloire de Dijon roses that Irma brought in from the garden, and another of white lilies. She was always washing her hands. She used a strange soap, after which her hands gave off a remotely exotic scent. To Irma, gradually, this scent began to stand for Mrs. Bronson: her frothy prettiness, her painting, the miraculous marital state.

In this way the natural heroine-worship sprang up. Just as Mrs. Harris saw herself in Irma, so Irma began to wish that she could see herself in Mrs. Bronson. She wanted to be able to do the things Mrs. Bronson did: to paint water-colours, to mix extraordinary oils for salad, to speak with her accent, to wash with that same remarkable soap. She did her best to dress a little like Mrs. Bronson. Instead of sitting with her hands outspread, like flowers, she began to sit with her arms crossed and her hands on their opposite shoulders, in the same bemused pretty attitude as Mrs. Bronson did.

All the time Mrs. Harris was watching. Years of financial alertness, of swift concentration against the remote chance of mistaking sixpence for a farthing, had left her eyes virtually lidless. She missed nothing. Her concentration on money was part instinctive, part habitual, part a fear of Harris's memory. Built up on farthings, Harris's financial success, by which he had been able to invest in the rows of working-class houses from which Irma and she now drew income, reproached her. Inspired in this way, she missed less than Harris himself. Her concentration on money had become a creed.

Similarly her concentration on Irma

was becoming a disease. For years it had been a kind of nervousness, some sort of chronic palsied illusion. As she saw Irma begin to model herself on Mrs. Bronson, it began to grow infinitely worse, more vicious, aggravated by the fact that, for once in her life, Irma was doing something outside the rule of the glass case. Having worshipped Irma all her life, it seemed beyond her comprehension that Irma could be guilty of worship in turn.

Mrs. Harris could not understand. She saw any affection between the two girls as beyond and without reason. She saw Irma captured by someone else, taken away from her. There was something unusual, fishy, not straight about it. In a fit of jealousy she tried to stop it.

"If I were you, I shouldn't bother Mrs. Bronson so much. You see, well, people like to be private. I don't think she wants you in there from morning to night."

In meek obedience, Irma stopped going into Mrs. Bronson's room. Mrs. Bronson at once noticed it.

"Why doesn't Irma come in to see me?"

Mrs. Harris was in a quandary. No use offending Mrs. Bronson. She didn't want to lose the Bronsons. An officer and his wife were better than three privates. It would pay her to be nice to Mrs. Bronson.

So Irma went back, and the natural friendship seemed if anything a little stronger, more easy, so that Irma tried apeing Mrs. Bronson not only in things like soap and dresses, but in thought and mannerisms. They naturally talked about Bronson, and once or twice Irma went in to have supper with them, and once Bronson teased her about her hair.

"You've got so much hair you ought to dish it out to the officers. One lock, one officer. You know, to put in his Bible next to his heart. It's not fair, one girl having enough hair for a regiment and keeping it."

It was just Bronson's joke, and they all enjoyed it.

Then, once or twice, Bronson and his wife took Irma for a walk after supper. They felt a little sorry for her, sensing the situation, seeing her under the domination of the mother, the scrubbed house, the fusty passages. "The poor kid's never had a chance. I feel a bit sorry for her," Mrs. Bronson said. And the three of them would walk out as far as the park, in the summer dusk, under the limes, and once Mrs. Bronson, who wore no hat, said she could feel the honey-dew falling from the lime leaves down on her hair. "Just trying to make it curl like Irma's," Bronson teased.

To Mrs. Harris it was all incomprehensible. Fretted by jealousy, her mind could not rest. It remained nervous, discontented, without power to do anything.

Then she saw what she took to be an extraordinary thing. Irma and the Bronsons had been for an evening walk. Five minutes after they were back, she saw Irma's straw hat and Bronson's cap lying in the same chair in the hall.

Not hung up, but thrown down, and together. Not Mrs. Bronson's hat. Irma's hat. With Bronson's thrown down in a hurry. At night, under cover of darkness.

Her mind gathered the nervous power and the direction it had lacked and shot off, before she could do anything, straight to Bronson. It seemed to hit Bronson with its extraordinary charge of suspicion, and then recoil back, leaving Mrs. Harris with the hot shell of staggered conviction in her hands.

It was Mr. Bronson. Not Mrs. Bronson. Mr. Bronson. Bronson! Her mind juggled with the red-hot conviction as a man juggles with the potato too hot to hold. Tossing it up and down, lacking the nerve to hold it, she was too distraught, that night, to do anything about it, and she kept up her distressed juggling performance all night, not knowing whether to be ashamed for Irma or enraged with Bronson, or both.

In the morning she had decided. For various reasons she would speak to Irma. There was the reason of money, the necessity of not offending the Bronsons. Then there was the reason that was much nearer Irma. Something had happened to Irma and it was very likely that Irma, a young girl, did not fully understand it.

"Irma," she said. "I want to speak to you." Then at the moment of crisis she felt her courage crumble. She felt that she could not say what she had to say in bare words, all pat, like a speech.

At this moment she remembered Harris. He, like the Lord, had had a weakness for speaking in parables. She would speak in a parable, and her idea of a parable was to say:

"Irma, you want to keep yourself to yourself."

Distress unexpectedly charged her voice with passion. The girl was wide-eyed, not understanding. She did not speak.

Mrs. Harris took silence for guilt. Her mind seized the hot charge of conviction and held it painfully but in spite of pain.

"Irma! Irma!"

"But mother, what's the matter?"

"What's the matter! That's a nice thing. As if you don't know. Oh! Irma, Irma. After all I've done for you, after the way I've brought you up." And then suddenly the plain accusation, final and incontrovertible, as if she needed nothing more than the two hats, Irma's and Bronson's, on a chair, and the girl's silence.

"Irma, you're running after Lieutenant Bronson! I won't have it. I've seen it! I know. I won't have it!"

The girl was still silent. To Mrs. Harris it seemed only like a confession, and in a way she was glad that it was all over so simply.

"That's all I've got to say — now. But I'd be ashamed of myself, Irma Harris. I would. I'd be utterly ashamed of myself."

Irma began to go about vaguely, for the first time in her life caught up by a dream of substantial reality. Up to that time she had not thought of Bronson. It was only Mrs. Bronson. She felt excitably affectionate towards Mrs. Bronson, virginally, tenderly, longing to be like her. Bronson had not touched her.

She began now to think of Bronson. What had her mother seen? She must have seen something. Knowing that she had never looked at Bronson, the girl could only wonder if Bronson had looked at her.

She began to try to figure it out for herself, in bed at night. She took the false premise of her mother, the accusation, and built up about it the arguments for one side and another, singling out the moments when she felt that there might have been something in Bronson's way of looking at her. She tried to argue it out impartially with herself, trying to prove there was nothing in it. And gradually, all the time, she was aware of an increasing feeling that it would be nice if it could be proved the other way. Then she wanted it proved the other way. She wanted to feel that Bronson had looked at her. She wanted to know, and even if necessary against all reason, that there was something in it after all.

Then all at once she thought of the things Bronson had said about her hair. Said jokingly, they suddenly took on the weight of great importance. She was staggered by them. Where they had seemed very trivial, not to be taken seriously, they now began to seem not only extraordinarily important, but very beautiful. As she lay stretched out in bed, she felt that all argument had ceased to have meaning. There was now no argument, no complexity. It was all different. The street lamp was still shining on the ceiling from outside, and looking up at it, she felt herself flooded by waves and waves of incandescent beauty. Borne on light, they were at the same time like intransient cadences of prolonged music. Sentimentally and passively she let them wash over her, and then recede, leaving her mind as clear-washed as a shore after a tide, smoothed and quiet, animated only by the faint phosphorescence of an absurd sort of rapture.

Subsequently she became almost awfully aware of Bronson's nearness. She went upstairs and met him coming down; took in the Bronsons' meals and stood while he took the dishes from her, almost touching her. She was aware on those occasions of flashes of extraordinarily electric emotion, part pleasure, part pain, and at nights she put on, in her mind, the gramophone record of things he had said to her or about her, letting herself be passively swirled away from the eternal revolutions of repeated thought.

Then Mrs. Harris noticed something else: the soap. Irma's soap was the same, she suddenly discovered, as Mrs. Bronson's soap.

That could only mean one thing.

It was an awful, outrageous thing. Soap, scent, the scent of hands and body and face: together they drove her to the edge of impossible conjecture.

She rushed straight up to Irma's bedroom, only to find the girl standing there by the window, looking at Bronson, drilling No. 3 Platoon farther down the street. For a moment Mrs. Harris could not speak. It was a moment of both humiliation and triumph. She felt enraged and yet quite strengthless. Then, before she could speak, Irma turned away from the window, lifted up her head and walked out of the room. She was a little flushed, but quite calm, and she did not speak.

Irma's look of unsubmissive tranquillity, her air of touch-me-not complacency, so beautiful and self-conscious and infuriating, aroused in Mrs. Harris a curious sort of enmity. Her synonymity with Irma was shattered. Irma had become another being, separate, unacknowledgeable, behaving with a self-confessed awful immorality that was a condemnation of Mrs. Harris herself.

Going downstairs, she followed Irma about, arguing, basing everything on that point. "What about me? What do you think I feel? After all I've done for you. Don't you see how I must feel? Don't you ever think of me? Don't you see how it affects me?"

The girl could not say anything. In so intangible an affair, where so much was only the fiction of the mind, there was nothing much she could do except be silent.

It was in silence that Mrs. Harris saw guilt. She blamed Irma bitterly, but only Irma, seeing her part in the affair as active, not passive. Irma was committing — staring out of the window, aping Mrs. Bronson, using the same soap — a wilful and stupid folly, a slight against parental decency. "Your father would have been *ashamed* of you." But it had not occurred to her that the Lieutenant might be condoning it.

Pushed farther into secrecy, Irma enlarged in her mind the small fiction of herself and Bronson. She was pushed back into an inward loneliness, in which she made a structure of one improbability built on another. These improbabilities, as they grew up pagoda-fashion, she began to see as solid truths, lighting them up with the shimmering adolescent light of her own fancy. In this beautiful abstract fashion, she persuaded herself into an intense belief in the reality of Bronson's affection for her, suffering with a certain pleasure, believing in the aspects of its tragedy as readily as she believed in its extraordinary ecstasy.

In the Bronson's room downstairs there was a large black tin case. Here Bronson kept his full-dress uniform, sword and various accoutrements. One night Irma cut off some of her hair and went downstairs, intending to put the hair into the breast-pocket of one of Bronson's tunics. In the darkness the lid of the box slipped out of her hands and crashed.

The Bronsons' bedroom was immediately above, and Bronson heard the crash and came downstairs. He switched on the electric light and saw Irma standing beside the box, in her nightgown. He had come down hurriedly, without a dressing-gown, and for a moment he was too embarrassed to speak. Irma stood trembling. Then just as he was going to speak he heard a door open upstairs, and he knew Mrs. Harris was coming down.

Something made him put out the light. In complete silence, he and the girl stood in the darkness, trying to deny each other's existence. They heard Mrs. Harris shuffle downstairs in her carpet slippers, and after about thirty seconds Bronson felt her hand stab at the light.

The words were ready on Mrs. Harris's lips, like bullets waiting to be fired. They exploded straight at Bronson, rapid-firing: "I got you. I caught you. I got you, I caught you."

Neither Bronson nor Irma could speak. Mrs. Harris took silence for guilt. She swivelled round and fired a double shot upstairs:

"Mrs. Bronson! Mrs. Bronson!"

Bronson stood white, tragically silent. He heard his wife's voice in reply and her movements as she came downstairs. He stood quiet, more nervous than Irma, still not saying anything, aware of his predicament and yet doing nothing, seeing himself only as the victim of some unhappy and apparently unchaste circumstance over which he had no control.

Mrs. Harris fired a fusillade of bitter triumph as Mrs. Bronson came and stood in the light of the doorway:

"They ain't moved, they ain't said nothing. That's how I found 'em. In their nightgowns. That's how I found 'em. I knew it had been going on for a long time, but not like this, not like this!"

Irma began to cry. Bronson and his wife stood with a kind of paste-board rigidity, stiffened by some inherent aristocratic impulse not to give way before people out of their class. They knew they had nothing to fear, yet they saw themselves confronted by the iron suspicion of Mrs. Harris as by a firing squad. In Mrs. Harris's small distracted grey eyes there was a touch of madness, inspired by triumph. She spoke with the rapid incoherence of someone sent slightly insane by a terrible discovery. "I don't know what you're going to do, but I know what I'm going to do. I know and I'm going to do it. If you're not ashamed, I am. I'm ashamed. I'm — "

At this moment Irma fainted.

"No wonder! No wonder! Gettin' her down here in her nightgown, on the sly. Gettin' her down here — "

The insane dangerous stupidity of it all only struck the Bronsons into dead silence. And in silence, as never before, Mrs. Harris saw guilt.

The next afternoon the Bronsons moved to other quarters. Irma, shut up in her room, heard Lieutenant Bronson's large tin box go clanking out of the hall like a coffin.

In less than a month there was hardly a soldier left in the town. In the papers Irma read about the regiment going to the Dardanelles, and read Bronson's name, a little later, among the killed.

More than two years later she read how Mrs. Bronson too had been killed. In Mexico, where she had gone to clear up some of Bronson's affairs, she had been hit, while sitting in a café, by a stray bullet in a local revolution.

Irma envied Mr. and Mrs. Bronson, the dead. She began to feel that she was going about with a bullet in her own heart, and was only gradually beginning to understand, by the pain of longer silences between herself and her mother, who had fired it.

A Funny Thing

MY Uncle Silas and my Uncle Cosmo belonged to different worlds; but they were men of identical kidney. Uncle Cosmo was a small man of dapper appearance with waxed moustaches who wore a gold ring on his right hand and a wine-coloured seal on his gold watchchain, and a green homburg hat. He carried a saucy silver-topped walking-stick and smoked cigars and looked exactly what he was: a masher. If Uncle Silas was the black sheep of one side of the family, Uncle Cosmo was the black sheep of the other. He habitually did an awful thing for which, I think, nobody ever forgave him: he spent his winters abroad. He sent us picture-postcards, then, of orange-trees in Mentone, the bay at Naples, Vesuvius, the gondolas of Venice, of himself in a straw hat on Christmas day at Pompeii, and wrote, airily: 'On to Greece and Port Said to-morrow, before the final jaunt to

71

Ceylon.' He was reputed, though nobody pretended so, to have a fancy lady in Nice, and there was something about a scandal in Colombo. Returning home in the spring of every year, he brought us oranges fresh from the bough, Sicilian pottery, oriental cushions, shells from the South Seas, lumps of gold-starred quartz and the war axes of aboriginal chieftains, and advice on how to eat spaghetti. He twiddled his seal and told amazing stories of hot geysers on remote southern islands and bananas at twenty-a-penny and how he had almost fought a duel with a Prussian in Cairo. Cosmopolitan, debonair, a lady-killer, Uncle Cosmo was altogether very impressive.

The only person not impressed by Cosmo was my Uncle Silas.

"You bin a long way, Cosmo," he would say, "but you ain't done much."

"Who hasn't? I've travelled over half the globe, Silas, while you sit here and grow prize gooseberries."

"I daresay," Silas said, "I daresay. But we only got your word for it. For all we know you might stop the winter in a boardin' house at Brighton."

"Silas," Uncle Cosmo said, "I could tell you stories of places between here and Adelaide that would make your liver turn green. Places — "

"Well, tell us then. Nobody's stoppin' you."

"I'm telling you. Here's just one thing. There's a desert in Assyria that's never been trodden by the foot of man and that's so far across it would take you three years to cross it on a camel. Now, one day — "

"You ever bin across this desert?"

"No, but — "

"Then how the hell d'ye know it takes three years to cross?"

"Well, it's — "

"What I thought," Silas said. "Just what I thought. You *hear* these things, Cosmo, you hear a lot, and you've bin a long way, but you ain't done much. Now, take women."

"Ah!"

"What about this fancy affair in Nice?"

"I haven't got a fancy affair in Nice!"

"There you are. Just what I thought. Big talk and nothing doing."

"She lives in Monte Carlo!"

"Well, that ain't so wonderful."

His pride wounded, Uncle Cosmo took a deep breath, drank a mouthful of my Uncle Silas's wine as though it were rat poison, pulled his mouth into shape again and said: "You don't seem to grasp it. It's not only one woman, Silas, in Monte Carlo. There's another in Mentone and another in Marseilles and two in Venice. I've got another who lives in an old palace in Naples, two I can do what I like with in Rome, a Grecian girl in Athens and two little Syrians in Port Said. They all eat out of my hand. Then, there's a niece of a Viscount in Colombo and a Norwegian girl in Singapore, and I forget whether its four or five French girls in Shanghai. Then of course in Japan — "

"Wait a minute," Silas said. "I thought you went abroad for your health?"

"Then in Hong Kong there's a Russian girl who's got a tortoise tattooed on her — "

"Well, there ain't nothing wonderful in that, either. Down at The Swan in Harlington there used to be a barmaid with a cuckoo or something tattooed on — "

74

"Yes, it was a cuckoo," Uncle Cosmo said. "I know, because I got her to have it done. She liked me. Yes, it was a cuckoo. And that's why they always used to say you could see the cuckoo earlier in Harlington than anywhere else in England."

My Uncle Silas was not impressed. He took large sardonic mouthfuls of wine, cocked his bloodshot eye at the ceiling and looked consistently sceptical, wicked and unaffected. When Uncle Cosmo then proceeded to relate the adventure of the two nuns in Bologna, my Uncle Silas capped it with the adventure of the three Seventh Day Adventists in a bathing hut at Skegness. When Uncle Cosmo told the story of how, in his shirt, he had been held up at the point of a pistol by a French husband in Biarritz, my Uncle Silas brought out the chestnut of how a gamekeeper had blown his hat off with a double-barrelled gun in Bedfordshire. The higher my Uncle Cosmo flew, the better my Uncle Silas liked it. "Did I ever tell you," Uncle Cosmo said, "of the three weeks I spent in a château in Arles with the wife of a French count?"

"No," Silas said. "But did I ever tell you of the month I spent with the duchess's daughter in Stoke Castle? The Hon. Lady Susannah. You can remember her?"

"Well, I — how long ago was this?"

"This was the winter of 'ninety-three. You ought to remember her. She used to ride down to Harlington twice a week, with a groom in a dog cart. Used to wear a black cloak with a splashed red lining."

"Dark girl?"

"That's her. Black. Long black hair and black eyes and long black eyelashes. A dazzler."

"Well, Silas, now you come to say, I — "

"Now wait a minute, Cosmo. You know what they used to say about this girl?"

"Well — "

"Never looked at a man in her life," my Uncle Silas said. "Never wanted to. Cold as a frog. Nobody couldn't touch her. Chaps had been after her from everywhere — London, all over the place. Never made no difference,

76

Cosmo. She just sat in the castle and looked out of the window and painted pictures. See?"

"Well, I — "

"You know the castle at Stoke? Stands down by the river."

"Oh, yes, Silas. Very well, very well."

"The grounds run right down to the river," Silas said. "Well, that winter I'd been doing a little river-poaching down there — eel lines and jack-snaring. You know? And about six o'clock one morning I was coming along under the castle wall with about thirty eels in a basket when she copped me."

"Who?"

"Her. The gal. She was sitting in a gateway in the wall with her easel, painting. It was just agettin' light and she told me afterwards she was painting the dawn over the river. 'You been poaching,' she said. Well, what could I say? I was done. She had me red-handed and she knew it."

"What did she do?"

"Well, Cosmo, she done a funny thing. She says, 'I won't say nothing about this business if you'll come up to the castle and let me paint your picture just as you are. Old clothes and eels and everything.' So I says, 'It's a go', and we went up to the castle and she began to paint the picture straight away that morning. 'The whole family's away abroad for the winter, and I'm all alone here except for the groom and butler,' she says. 'And after today you come along every morning and catch your eels and then come up to the castle and let me paint you.'"

And my Uncle Silas went on to relate, between wry mouthfuls of wine, how for more than a week he had done as she said, trapping the eels in the early morning and going up to the castle and slipping in by a side door and letting the girl paint him in her room. Until at last something happened. It rained torrentially for a whole day and the succeeding night and when he went down to the river on the following morning he found the floods up and the small stone cattle bridge leading over to the castle smashed by water. It meant a detour of six miles and it was almost eight o'clock by the time he reached the castle. He slipped in by the side door as usual and went upstairs and into the girl's room, and there standing before a cheval mirror, the girl was painting a picture of herself in the nude.

"And that just about finished it?" Cosmo said.

"No, Cosmo, that just about began it."

"Well," Cosmo said, "what did she do?"

"A funny thing, Cosmo," my Uncle Silas said, "a funny thing. She just went on painting. "I thought you weren't coming," she says, "so I got on with this picture of myself. You like it?" Well, I was standing so as I could see the back of her in the flesh, the sideways of her in the picture and the front of her in the mirror, and I was flummoxed. "Well," she says, "perhaps you don't like it because it isn't finished? Let me put my clothes on and let's have some fried eels and you tell me what you think of it."

So my Uncle Silas went on to say they had fried eels and talked about the picture and he said something about not being able to judge the picture on such short acquaintance with the model. "You'll see me again to-morrow," she said, and so it went on: she painting herself in the nude, Silas watching, until at last, as Silas himself said, a month had gone by and he'd caught almost every eel in the river.

"You heard me say she was cold?" he said. "Never looked at a man and never wanted one? That's a fairy tale, Cosmo. Don't you believe it. It's true she never looked at men. But she looked at one man. And you know who that was."

"And what stopped it?" Cosmo said.

"What stopped it? A funny thing, Cosmo, a funny thing. There were twenty bedrooms in the castle, and we slept in every one of 'em. Then, one night, I was a little fuzzled and I must have gone into the wrong room. As soon as I got in I saw her in bed with another man. She gave one shout. "My husband!" she says, and I ran like greased lightning and down the drainpipe. The funny thing is she wasn't married, and never was, and I never did find out who the chappie was."

"You never found out," Uncle Cosmo said.

"No," Silas said. "I never did find out."

"Well," Cosmo said, "it's been a long time ago and I daresay it wouldn't break my heart to tell you. I happen to know, Silas, who that man was."

"You do?"

"I do."

"Well," Silas said, "who was it?"

Uncle Cosmo took a deep breath and twiddled his waxed moustaches and tried to look at once repentant and triumphant. "Silas," he said, "I hate to say it. I hate it. But it was me."

For about a minute my Uncle Silas did not speak. He cocked his eye and looked out of the window; he looked down at the wine in his glass; and then finally he looked across at Uncle Cosmo himself.

"Cosmo," he says at last, "you bin a long way and you've heard a tidy bit, but you ain't seen much. Don't you know there ain't a castle at Stoke? Nor a river?"

Uncle Cosmo did not speak.

"And don't you know where you was

81

in the winter o' 'ninety-three?"

Uncle Cosmo did not speak.

"Didn't you tell me only yesterday," Silas said, with his hand on the wine, "you was in Barbadoes that year, a bit friendly with a bishop's daughter? Now ain't that a funny thing?"

Château Bougainvillaea

THE headland was like a dry purple island scorched by the flat heat of afternoon, cut off from the mainland by a sand-coloured tributary of road which went down past the estaminet and then, half a mile beyond, to the one-line, one-eyed railway station. Down below, on a small plateau between upper headland and sea, peasants were mowing white rectangles of corn. The tide was fully out, leaving many bare black rocks and then a great sun-phosphorescent pavement of sand, with the white teeth of small breakers slowly nibbling in. Far out, the Atlantic was waveless, a shade darker than the sky, which was the fierce blue seen on unbelievable posters. Farther out still, making a faint mist, sun and sea had completely washed out the line of sky.

From time to time a puff of white steam, followed by a peeped whistle, struck comically at the dead silence

83

inland. It was the small one-line train, half-tram, making one way or the other its hourly journey between town-terminus and coast. By means of it the engaged couple measured out the afternoon.

"There goes the little train," he would say.

"Yes," she would say, "there goes the little train."

Each time she resolved not to say this stupid thing and then, dulled with sleepiness and the heat of earth and sky and the heather in which they lay, she forgot herself and said it, automatically. Her faint annoyance with herself at these times had gradually begun to make itself felt, as the expression of some much deeper discontent.

"Je parle Français un tout petit peu, m'sieu." In a voice which seemed somehow like velvet rubbed the wrong way, the man was talking. "I was all right as far as that. Then I said, 'Mais, dites-moi, m'sieu, pourquoi are all the knives put left-handed dans ce restaurant?' By God it must have been awfully funny. And then he said — "

"He said because, m'sieu, the people

who use them are all left-handed."

"And that's really what he said? It wasn't a mistake? All the people in that place were left-handed?"

"Apparently," she said, "they were all left-handed."

"It's the funniest thing I ever heard," he said. "I can't believe it."

Yes, she thought, perhaps it was a funny thing. Many left-handed people staying at one restaurant. A family, perhaps. But then there were many left-handed people in the world, and perhaps, for all you knew, their left was really right, and it was we, the right, who were wrong.

She took her mind back to the restaurant down in the town. There was another restaurant there, set in a sort of alley-way under two fig-trees, where artisans filled most of the tables between noon and 2 o'clock, and where a fat white-smocked woman served all the dishes and still found time to try her three words of English on the engaged couple. From here they could see the lace-crowned Breton women clacking in the shade of the street trees and the small one-eyed train starting or ending its journey between the sea and the terminus that was simply the middle of the street. They liked this restaurant, but that day, wanting a change, they had climbed the steps into the upper town, to the level of the viaduct, and had found this small family restaurant where, at one table, all the knives were laid left-handed. For some reason she now sought to define, this left-handedness did not seem funny to her. Arthur had also eaten too many olives, picking them up with his fingers and gnawing them as she herself, as a child, would have gnawed an uncooked prune, and this did not seem very funny either. Somewhere between olives and left-handedness lay the source of her curious discontent. Perhaps she was left-handed herself? Left-handed people were, she had read somewhere, right-brained. Perhaps Arthur was left-handed?

She turned over in the heather, small brown-eyed face to the sun. "Don't you do anything left-handed?"

"Good gracious, no." He turned over too and lay face upwards, dark with sun, his mouth small-lipped under the stiff moustache she had not wanted him to grow. "You don't either?"

For the first time in her life she considered it. How many people, she thought, ever considered it? Thinking, she seemed to roll down a great slope, semi-swooning in the heat, before coming up again. Surprisingly, she had thought of several things.

"Now I come to think of it, I comb my hair left-handed. I always pick flowers left-handed. And I wear my watch on my left wrist."

He lifted steady, mocking eyes. "You sure you don't kiss left-handed?"

"That's not very funny!" she flashed.

It seemed to her that the moment of temper flashed up sky high, like a rocket, and fell far out to sea, soundless, dead by then, in the heat of the unruffled afternoon. She at once regretted it. For five days now they had lived on the Breton coast, and they now had five days more. Every morning, for five days, he had questioned her: "All right? Happy?" and every morning she had responded with automatic affirmations, believing it at first, then aware of doubt, then bewildered. Happiness, she wanted to say, was not something you could fetch out every morning after breakfast, like a clean handkerchief, or more still like a rabbit conjured out of the hat of everyday circumstances.

The hot, crushed-down sense of security she had felt all afternoon began suddenly to evaporate, burnt away from her by the first explosion of discontent and then by small restless flames of inward anger. She felt the growing sense of insecurity physically, feeling that at any moment she might slip off the solid headland into the sea. She suddenly felt a tremendous urge, impelled for some reason by fear, to walk as far back inland as she could go. The thought of the Atlantic far below, passive and yet magnetic, filled her with a sudden cold breath of vertigo.

"Let's walk," she said.

"Oh! no, it's too hot."

She turned her face into the dark sun-brittled heather. She caught the ticking of small insects, like infinitesimal watches. Far off, inland, the little train cut off, with its comic shriek, another section of afternoon.

In England he was a draper's assistant: chief assistant, sure to become manager. In imagination she saw the shop, sun-blinds down, August remnant sale now on, the dead little town now so foreign and far off and yet so intensely real to her, shown up by the disenchantment of distance. They had been engaged six months. She had been very thrilled about it at first, showing the ring all round, standing on a small pinnacle of joy, ready to leap into the tremendous spaces of marriage. Now she had suddenly the feeling that she was about to be sewn up in a blanket.

"Isn't there a castle," she said, "somewhere up the road past the estaminet?"

"Big house. Not castle."

"I thought I saw a notice," she said, "to the château."

"Big house," he said. "Did you see that film, 'The Big House'? All about men in prison."

What about women in prison? she wanted to say. In England she was a school-teacher, and there had been times when she felt that the pale green walls of the class-room had imprisoned her and that marriage, as it always did, would mean escape. Now left-handedness and olives and blankets and the stabbing heat of the Atlantic afternoon had succeeded, together, in inducing some queer stupor of semi-crazy melancholy that was far worse than this. Perhaps it was the wine, the sour red stuff of the *vin compris* notice down at the left-handed café? Perhaps after all, it was only some large dose of self-pity induced by sun and the emptiness of the day?

She got to her feet. "Come on, m'sieu. We're going to the castle." She made a great effort to wrench herself up to the normal plane. "Castle, my beautiful. Two francs. All the way up to the castle, two francs." She held out her hand to pull him to his feet.

"I'll come," he said, "if we can stop at the estaminet and have a drink."

"We'll stop when we come down," she said.

"Now."

"When we come down."

"Now. I'm so thirsty. It was the olives."

Not speaking, she held out her hand. Instinctively, he put out his left.

"You see," she said, "you don't know what's what or which's which or anything. You don't know when you're left-handed or right."

He laughed. She felt suddenly like laughing too, and they began to walk down the hill. The fierce heat seemed itself to force them down the slope, and she felt driven by it past the blistered white tables of the estaminet with the fowls asleep underneath them, and then up the hill on the far side, into the sparse shade of small wind-levelled oaks and, at one place, a group of fruitless fig trees. It was some place like this, she thought, just about as hot and arid, where the Gadarene swine had stampeded down. What made her think of that? Her mind had some urge towards inconsequence, some inexplicable desire towards irresponsibility that she could not restrain or control, and she was glad to see the château at last, shining with sea-blue jalousies through a break in the mass of metallic summer-hard leaves of acacia and bay that surrounded it. She felt it to be something concrete, a barrier against which all the crazy irresponsibilities of the mind could hurl themselves and split.

At the corner, a hundred yards before the entrance gates, a notice, of which one end had been cracked off by a passing lorry, pointed upwards like a tilted telescope. They read the word 'château', the rest of the name gone.

"You see," she said, "château."

"What château?"

"Just château."

"You think we'll have to pay to go in?"

"I'll pay," she said.

She walked on in silence, far away from him. The little insistences on money had become, in five days, like the action of many iron files on the soft tissues of her mind: first small and fine, then larger, then still larger, now large and coarse, brutal as stone. He kept a small note-book and in it, with painful system, entered up the expenditure of every centime.

At the entrance gates stood a lodge, very much delapidated, the paintwork of the walls grey and sea-eroded like the sides of a derelict battleship. A small notice was nailed to the fence by the gate, and the girl stopped to read it.

"What does it say?" he said. "Do we pay to go in?"

"Just says it's an eighteenth-century château," she said. "Admission a franc. Shall we go in?"

"A franc?"

"One franc," she said. "Each."

"You go," he said. "I don't know that I'm keen. I'll stop outside."

She did not answer, but went to the gate and pulled the porter's bell. From the lodge door a woman without a blouse on put her head out, there was a smell of onions, and the woman turned on the machine of her French like a high pressure steam-pipe, scrawny neck dilating.

The girl pushed open the gate and paid the woman the two francs admission fee, holding a brief conversation with her. The high pressure pipe finally cut itself off and withdrew, and the girl came back to the gates and said: "She's supposed to show us round but she's just washing. She says nobody else ever comes up at this hour of the afternoon, and we must show ourselves round."

They walked up the gravel road between sea-stunted trees towards the château. In the sun, against the blue sky above the Atlantic, the stone and slate of it was burning.

"Well," she said, "what do you think of it?"

"Looks a bit like the bank at home," he said. "The one opposite our shop."

Château and sky and trees spun in the sun-light, whirling down to a momentary black vortex in which the girl found herself powerless to utter a word. She walked blindly on in silence. It was not until they stood under the château walls, and she looked up to see a great grape vine mapped out all across the south side, that she recovered herself and could speak.

"Its just like the châteaux you see on wine-bottles," she said. "I like it."

"It doesn't look much to me," he said. "Where do we get in?"

"Let's look round the outside first."

As they walked round the walls on the sun-bleached grass she could not speak or gather her impressions, but was struck only by the barren solitude of it all, the arid, typically French surroundings, with an air of fly-blownness and sun weariness. To her amazement the place had no grandeur, and there were no flowers.

"There ought to be at least a bougainvillaea," she said.

"What's a bougainvillaea?"

Questioned, she found she did not know. She felt only that there ought to be a bougainvillaea. The word stood in her mind for the exotic, the south, white afternoons, the sea as seen from the top of just such châteaux as this. How this came to be she could not explain. The conscious part of herself stretched out arms and reached back, into time, and linked itself with some former incarnation of her present self, Louise Bowen, school-teacher, certificated, Standard V girls, engaged to Arthur Keller, chief assistant Moore's Drapery, sure to become manager, pin-stripe trousers, remnants madam, the voice like ruffled velvet, seventy-three pounds fifteen standing to credit at the post office, and in reaching back so far she felt suddenly that she could

95

cry for the lost self, for the enviable incarnation so extraordinarily real and yet impossible, and for the yet not impossible existence, far back, in eternal bougainvillaea afternoons.

"Let's go inside," she said.

"How they make it pay," he said, "God only knows."

"It has long since," she said mysteriously, "paid for itself."

They found the main door and went in, stepping into the under-sea coldness of a large entrance hall. Now think that out, now think that out, now think that out. Her mind bubbling with bitterness, she looked up the great staircase, and all of a sudden the foreignness of her conscious self as against the familiarity of the self that had been was asserted again, but now with the sharp contrast of shadow and light. She put her hand on the staircase, the iron cool and familiar, and then began to walk up it, slowly but lightly, her hand drawn up easily, as though from some invisible iron pulley, far above her. She kept her eyes on the ceiling, feeling, without effort of thought, that she did not like and never had liked its mournful collection of cherubim painted in the gold wheel about the chandelier. For the first time that day, as she mounted the staircase and then went on beyond into the upstairs corridor, and into the panelled music-room with its air of having been imported as a complete back-cloth from some pink-and-gold theatre of the seventies, her body moved with its natural quietness, accustomed, infinitely light, and with a sense of the purest happiness. All this she could not explain and, as they went from music-room to other rooms, ceased to attempt to explain. Her bitterness evaporated in the confined coolness just as her security, out-outside on the hot headland, had evaporated in the blaze of afternoon. Now she seemed incontestably sure of herself, content in what she knew, without fuss, was an unrepeatable moment of time.

She did not like the music-room but, as she expected, Arthur did. This pre-awareness of hers saved her from fresh bitterness. As part of her contentment, making it complete, she thought of him with momentary tenderness, quietly regretting what she had said and done, ready now to make up for it.

"Shall we go up higher," she said, "or down to the ground-floor again?"

"Let's do the climb first," he said.

To her, it did not matter, and climbing a second staircase they came, eventually, to a small turret room, unfurnished, with two jalousied windows looking across to the two worlds of France and the Atlantic.

She stood at the window overlooking the sea and looked out, as from a lighthouse, down on to the intense expanse of sea-light. Her mind had the profound placidity of the sea itself, a beautiful vacancy, milkily restful.

"Funny," Arthur said. "No ships. The Atlantic, and not a ship in sight."

"You wouldn't expect to see ships," she said, and knew that she was right.

Looking down from the other window they saw the headland, the brown-lilac expanse of heather, the minute peasants scribbled on the yellow rectangle of corn, the estaminet, the one-eyed station. And suddenly also, there was the white pop of steam inland, and the small comic shriek, now more than ever toy-like, pricking the dead silence of afternoon.

"Look," he said, "there's the little train."

"Yes," she said, "there's the little train."

Her mind had the pure loftiness of the tower itself, above all irritation. She felt, as not before in her life, that she was herself. The knowledge of this re-incarnation was something she could not communicate, and half afraid that time or a word would break it up, she suggested suddenly that they should go down.

Arthur remained at the window a moment longer, admiring points of distance. "You'd never think," he said, "you could see so far."

"Yes you would," she called back.

Now think that out, now think that out, now think that out. Her mind, as she went downstairs, sprang contrarily upwards, on a scale of otherwise inexpressible delight. Arthur engaged her in conversation as they went downstairs, she on one flight, he on one above, calling down: "It may be all right, but the rates must be colossal. Besides you'd burn a ton of coal a day in winter, trying to keep warm. A six-roomed house is bad enough, but think of this," but nothing could break, suppress or even touch her mood.

Downstairs she went straight into the great reception hall, and stood dumb. At that moment she suddenly felt that she had come as far as she must. Time had brought her to this split second of itself simply in order to pin her down. She stood like an insect transfixed.

Arthur came in: "What are you looking at?"

"The yellow cloth. Don't do anything. Just look at it. It's wonderful."

"I don't see anything very wonderful," he said.

At the end of the room, thrown over a chair, a large length of brocade, the colour of a half-ripe lemon, was like spilled honey against the grey French-coldness of walls and furniture. Instantaneously the girl saw it with eyes of familiarity, feeling it somehow to be the expression of herself, mood, past and future. She stood occupied with the entrancement of the moment, her eyes excluding the room, the day, Arthur and everything, her self drowned out of existence by the pure wash of watered fabric.

Suddenly Arthur moved into the room, and ten seconds later had the brocade in his hands. She saw him hold it up, measure it without knowing he measured it, feel its weight, thickness, value. She saw him suddenly as the eternal shopkeeper measuring out the eternal remnants of time: the small tape-measure of his mind like a white worm in the precious expanse of her own existence.

"If you bought it to-day," Arthur called, "it would cost you every penny of thirty-five bob a yard."

"Let's go," she said.

Half a minute later she turned and walked out of the door, Arthur following, and then past the wind-stunted trees and on down the road, past the estaminet. It was now herself who walked, Louise Bowen, Standard V girls, certificated, deduct so much for superannuation scheme, tired as after a long day in the crowded chalk-smelling class-room. As they passed the estaminet, the place looked more fly-blown and deserted than ever, and they decided to go on to the station, and get a drink there while waiting for the train. As they passed the fig trees her mind tried to grasp again at the thought of the Gadarene swine, her mood blasted into the same barrenness as the tree in the parable.

"Well, you can have your château," Arthur said. "But I've got my mind on one of those houses Sparkes is putting up on Park Avenue. Sixteen and fourpence a week, no deposit, over twenty years. That's in front of any château."

She saw the houses as he spoke, red and white, white and red, millions of them, one like another, sixteen and fourpence a week, no deposit, stretching out to the ends of the earth. She saw herself in them, the constant and never-changing material of her life cut up by a pair of draper's scissors, the days ticketed, the years fretted by the counting up of farthings and all the endlessly incalculable moods of boredom.

"Two coffees please."

At the little station café they sat at

one of the outside tables and waited for the train.

"Well, we've been to the château and never found out its name," he said.

"It ought to be Château Bougainvillaea."

"That's silly," he said. "You don't even know what a bougainvillaea is."

She sat stirring the grey coffee. She could feel the sun burning the white iron table and her hands. She looked up at the château, seeing the windows of the turret above the trees.

"Now we can see the château," she said, "as we should have seen ourselves if we'd been sitting down here when — "

It was beyond her, and she broke off.

"What?" he said.

"I didn't mean that," she said.

"What did you mean?"

"I don't know."

"Well, in future," he said, "mind you say what you mean."

The future? She sat silent. Inland the approaching train made its comic little whistle, cutting off another section of the afternoon.

And hearing it, she knew suddenly that the future was already a thing of the past.

The Ship

MY aunt Franklin, a long time ago, kept a small shop on the top of the high pavement. My uncle Franklin, who was dead, had been a taxidermist. But it is not about either of them that I want to tell you. They had a son, Ephraim Franklin, a sailor.

Whenever I went to see my aunt Franklin she was sitting in the room behind the shop. This room and the shop were filled with cases of stuffed animals and fish and butterflies and in this gloomy north facing little room, always so dull that even the colours of the butterflies seemed like dusty paint and the eyes of the animals as dull as shoe buttons, my aunt Franklin would sit talking or thinking about her son. His ship was called *The Mary Porter* and she was a sailing ship, a square rigger. Her port was Greenock and she made a fairly regular passage to Australia, taking a hundred days, even a hundred and fifty days; or she would be outward bound for Singapore, to await new orders there, going down afterwards to New Guinea, or Java, or Celebes, or Sumatra, or Borneo. And so because of this, because it took *The Mary Porter* a hundred and fifty days out and perhaps a hundred and fifty days back, the most my Aunt Franklin could ever hope to see her son was once a year. And in the meantime, for two hundred and fifty or even three hundred days, all she thought of was Ephraim, anxiety for Ephraim, joy for Ephraim, Ephraim in the East Indies, Ephraim working hard to be second mate, Ephraim's photograph on the wall, until at last Ephraim himself came home, from the South Seas.

The first time I ever saw Ephraim I was about ten or eleven. I went to see my aunt on a cold mizzling November afternoon and there, in the back room, home from a voyage of a hundred and thirty-five days from Sydney, sat Ephraim. He was then the second mate of *The Mary Porter*, a big man with a thick ginger beard and ice-blue eyes and stiff ginger hair on the backs of his hands. He talked

105

to me all that afternoon; or rather he talked to my aunt, telling her stories. "Mother, they was twice as long as this room, these codfish. They'll eat a man, I tell you," or "Mother, I'd tell you about the Mokoru tribe in New Guinea only it'd turn your stomach before tea," or "Yes, Mother, next voyage it'll be first mate. First mate. Mister Franklin." And I listened to him all that afternoon as he sat picking bits of tobacco out of his teeth with a bodkin, his voice conjuring up for me the sight and smell of foreign parts, strange islands, *The Mary Porter* sailing beyond tropical horizons. He ate six soft-boiled eggs for tea that day, I shall always remember it, and then after tea he went upstairs and came down with a black tin box, carrying it by the handle. "Mother," he said, "I'll give you six guesses." So she sat there with her chin on her knuckles, an ivory-faced plain frail-looking little woman who looked the last person in the world to be the mother of a hairy second mate as big as he was, and guessed what it was he had brought her from the South Seas. She guessed a parrot, a pair of slippers, a comb, a shawl and then she gave it up. "No," he said, "wrong every time." It was an ivory box, carved with figures of fish and ships, and in it was a necklace of white coral. She loved them both and her face went as white as the coral and there were tears in her eyes. "Ah! you wait," he said, "one day I'll bring you summat worth bringing. I'll bring you a necklace of black pearls.

Black pearls. How's that, eh?" And suddenly he became aware of my standing there, listening and gaping at them both, and he said: "Here, son, you nip off now and come in to-morrow. You come in to-morrow and I'll show you the model I'm making of *The Mary Porter*."

The next day was Sunday and I could not go, but I went on Monday and he showed me the model of *The Mary Porter*. He had been making it for three voyages. When would it be finished? I said. "When will it be finished?" he said. "Oh! in about two more. I'll finish it before I get my master's ticket." I stayed looking at the model of *The Mary Porter* all that afternoon. It fascinated me. Already it was a lovely thing, built as though in a shipyard, from the keel up, faithful in every detail, even below decks, to the ship in which Ephraim sailed. "And next time I'm home," he said, "you'll see her rigging up, and then the next time she'll be carrying all her canvas." As he told me about her I could already see her, in my mind, as a lovely and complete thing. For the next five weeks I got a glimpse of her whenever I could, and then, the day before Ephraim sailed again, I looked at her for the last time. He caught me looking at her very longingly, and suddenly, as though thinking perhaps that I were jealous of his having brought me nothing from that last voyage, he said:

"Well, son, you be a good boy now and keep your nose tidy and you know what I'll do? Eh? You know what I'll do if you're a good boy? I'll bring you a nigger gal."

"Oh! Ephraim!" my aunt said, "saying bits like that to the boy."

"Ah, that's right, ain't it, son? You be a good boy and I'll bring you a black gal home. That's a promise, ain't it?"

He was so serious that I think, at

the time, I half believed him and then, over the nine months' interval of that next voyage, I forgot about it. What I thought of was the ship. I would think of her assuming, in Ephraim's hands, her full shape, and of the beautiful light airy look that the rigging would give her. I would think of Ephraim knotting that rigging down in his cabin, under the hanging oil-lamp, on hot black tropical nights, moving the little ship gradually and patiently to its moment of completion.

Ephraim came home again in the October of the following year. I forget what he brought his mother that time, but I know that, as he had promised, the rigging of *The Mary Porter* was finished and true in every detail. It gave the ship that wonderful, lofty air, quite magical, that sailing ships have when they carry no canvas. I marvelled at that ship and for five weeks looked at it whenever he would let me, until he must have known how I coveted it. I marvelled too at Ephraim's patience. "Yes," he said, "it takes a longish stretch. But then I'm working for my master's ticket and that takes up a lot o' time too. But I'll soon be finished with that now, I hope."

He was finished with it that very time ashore. He got his master's ticket in London that November and in December the owners of *The Mary Porter* gave him his first command. The ship was another square-rigger, older than *The Mary Porter*, and I forget her name. "And where will you be bound for?" I said.

"Singapore," he said, "and pick up fresh orders there."

He sailed in January, and the day before he sailed he let me look at the model of *The Mary Porter* again.

"Shall you be able to finish it now?" I said.

"Finish it? Easy. All I got to do is get the sails made and hoisted and I can do that with one hand tied behind my back."

"When'll you be home?" I said.

"Home? Never tell," he said. "But you know what I told you, don't you? You be a good boy and I'll bring you a nigger gal. That's right, ain't it? You be a good boy and I'll bring you a nice fat blackie.

She'll make your hair curl."

"Ephraim," my aunt said, "give over, do."

That time Ephraim was away nine months. My aunt did not know when he was coming home. She never knew. She would be sitting there in the back room, wondering if Ephraim were in the Bay of Biscay or the Indian Ocean or even at the bottom of the ocean, when suddenly the shop-bell would ring and a voice would shout, "Shop, missus!" and it would be Ephraim home again.

But when he came home that following November, from that first command, he came into the shop without a word. It was Saturday afternoon and I was there in the back room with her. When she heard the shop-bell ring she got up and went to the glass-panelled, curtain-screened door that divided shop from living room and she opened it. She opened it and then she just stood there. I heard her say 'Ephriam', and nothing else, in a not very loud voice. Then there was a silence, as though of completely stupefied astonishment. Then she went slowly forward into the shop. As she went forward I moved forward a few paces too. Through the still open door I could see Ephraim. There was someone with him. For a moment I could not see who it was, because aunt Franklin was standing there. Then she moved and I could see who it was. It was a woman. But for a moment I did not realize what woman or what sort of woman. Then suddenly, even in the bad light of the shop, I could see the colour of her face. It was black. For about ten seconds my heart stood still and I knew that Ephraim had brought home a black girl from the South Seas.

If I had any illusions about Ephraim having brought home that girl for me I know that they didn't last long. After about a minute Ephraim came slowly out of the shop into the back room. He was alone and he shut the door behind him. He did not seem to notice I was there. All he did was to put his hands on my aunt Franklin's shoulders and say: "Mother, it's all right. She's all right. Honest, she's the only gal I ever wanted. It'll be all right." But I knew, somehow, that it wasn't going to be all right. My aunt did not speak and she was crying.

Then, after a few moments, Ephraim noticed me. "Hullo, son," he said. "You run along now and come in another day. And don't go chopsing all over the place either."

I knew what that meant. I went away and I kept my mouth shut. But I remember, as I went out through the shop and passed the black girl still standing there looking at Ephraim and his mother through the lace curtains of the glass door, that I was suddenly frightened. Then it passed. She looked as completely scared as I was — scared and forlorn in the cheap high bandeau hat and blue serge costume that Ephraim must have bought her up in Glasgow.

That was my first picture of her, scared and forlorn and out of place. I did not see her again for more than a week. Then I saw her walking out with Ephraim in the High Street, and I saw then that she wasn't black, but brown, a soft, coffee-cream brown, with large, gentle eyes like ripe black grapes, and I thought she was lovely. Neither she nor Ephraim looked at me. They did not seem to look at anyone. They walked down that crowded Saturday evening High Street as though they were walking along the empty sea-shore of some remote New Guinea island, completely oblivious of everyone, infinitely happy.

But if they were oblivious of everyone there was no one in the town, from my aunt Franklin downwards, who was oblivious of them. People were all talking about the scandal of Ephraim Franklin bringing home a black girl and they all called her a nigger. Somehow it was a terrible, outrageous, wicked thing, and one day when I went into my aunt Franklin's shop I heard my aunt and Ephraim quarrelling in the back room, she arguing from just that standpoint, how terrible it was, how wicked it was, and he trying to soothe her: "Mother, she's only human, she's flesh and blood, she comes of very high class. It'll be better when she can speak English. You'll git along better then." But this remark seemed to upset my aunt still more. "That's it, that's the trouble. I shouldn't care if she could only speak to me!"

I went out of the shop, that day,

without going into the back room, and I did not go back any more for a fortnight. When I went back Ephraim was not there. He had gone to Greenock, I think, to see the owners. I think there had been some trouble, perhaps about the black girl. At any rate, when I went into the back room neither Ephraim nor my aunt was there. The black girl sat there all alone, in a plain blue, ready-made frock that didn't fit her. It was a dark December day, with raw rain, near Christmas, and she was trying to keep herself warm by the fire. I don't think she could have been more than eighteen, perhaps even less than that, and now, instead of looking scared, she looked pleased to see me, showing the pleasure in a sudden pure white smile. "Hullo," I said, and to my astonishment she said "Hullo" too.

Besides 'yes' and 'no' that was her only word of English. She kept repeating it. "Hulloyes," she would say, all in one word. Her voice was quite high, but smooth; it prolonged her three words of English to double their length, until they had a dreamy, mooning, regretful quality.

I don't think she really knew what any of them meant, any more than she really understood anything much about that gloomy little shop, with its dead fish and animals, and the still gloomier little room behind. It must all have been sepulchrally strange and foreign to her, not quite real, with the lead-coloured December light shining on the dead glass that covered the dead animals, and the dead light itself gradually being watered away by the dark December rain beyond the windows. It must have sent her thoughts flying back to wherever it was she came from, and it must, I think, have made her unhappy, because now and then you would see her look far beyond windows and rain and dark sky with a look of unconscious pain.

But there were two things in that room that she did understand. One was a case of butterflies; they were tropical and I think perhaps, at one time, Ephraim had brought them home for his father. The other was Ephraim's ship, the model of *The Mary Porter*.

Ephraim had brought home the ship for the last time. It was finished and

116

it stood on the mantelpiece above the fireplace. It stood raised up, on a wooden support, in front of a pier-glass. The glass was tilted so that, just now and then, you had the illusion of the ship, with all her canvas set, waiting for a breeze in the dead calm of some tropical latitude where sky and sea had fused to a sheet of glass.

And she understood that ship. She must have seen its original over and over again. It would provoke her into long moments of reflection, not painful, not really happy, but full of something inexpressible.

Nothing happened about the ship that afternoon. Soon after that first 'Hullo' my aunt came in with a bucket of small coal and kindling sticks that she had been chopping in the back-yard and as she set down the bucket by the fireplace she looked old and yellow, like a woman who has just come through an illness. She muttered something about not being so young as she used to be and another remark about some people who were young enough to do things but never lifted a finger, and I knew she was bitter against the black girl. Then I had an idea. "Let me come round every afternoon through the Christmas holidays," I said, "and get your sticks and coal in."

So I began to go round every afternoon, and sometimes Ephraim's black girl would be sitting there, by the fire, doing nothing except staring at the ship or the sky or the butterflies. And sometimes Ephraim himself would be there and they would be talking together, in her language, softly, this barrier of language cutting them off from my aunt, who would sit silent and apart from them, her yellow face bone-hard with an extraordinary bitterness and jealousy.

Then on the last day but one of December I went there and Ephraim had gone. He had sailed that day for Singapore, master of a ship named *The Border Lass*, for different owners I think, and he had left the black girl behind. He had left her because, I think, neither the new owners nor the old nor any others would ever countenance the sailing of a white skipper with a coloured wife. How he had ever brought her in the first place I could never fathom. Why

118

he had brought her was something which troubled my aunt still more.

And even I, a boy, could see what was going to happen. It would be nine months, perhaps longer, before Ephraim came back. And in the meantime? I could see nothing but tension: the tension of the long winter days in the gloomy room behind the shop, the girl with her three words of English able to express almost nothing of what she felt, my aunt expressing what she felt by jealousy and silence. I could see all this, but how it was going to end was beyond me.

Then something happened. Every Thursday afternoon my aunt shut the shop, and sometimes she took the train into the next town, to see some friends. One Thursday when I went round to the shop to get in the coal and sticks she had shut the shop and gone, leaving Ephraim's black girl alone in the back room.

"Hulloyes," she said when I went into the back room, and smiled.

"Hullo," I said.

I put the bucket of coal and sticks down by the fireplace, and then I didn't know what to say. Then suddenly she looked at the ship on the mantelpiece and said, "Ephraim?"

"Ah!" I said, "Ephraim on sea. Yes. Understand? On sea now. All right."

She didn't understand. She just looked at me with a large bewildered smile.

"Ephraim on sea," I said. "Understand?"

No, she didn't understand. So at least I got the ship down and knelt on the hearthrug and began to rock the ship backwards and forwards and up and down. She would be just about like that now, I thought, in the Bay of Biscay. The girl understood. She knelt down on the hearthrug and began to push the ship backwards and forwards across it, steering it. The way she pushed it was different from the way I pushed it. She pushed it softly, sleepily. I could see she meant it to be in calm latitudes. "Kimusa," she said. "Kimusa." Now it was I who didn't understand and I shook my head. So she reached up and got down a book from my aunt's little bookshelf made of boards and cotton-reels that hung by the fireplace and put the book down on the hearthrug. Then she sailed Ephraim's ship close by the book and pointed to the book again and said, "Kimusa." Then suddenly I tumbled to it. Kimusa was an island, her island. I nodded and she smiled again. She was quite excited. She sailed the ship close to the island and suddenly I saw what she was trying to tell me: that this was Ephraim in *The Mary Porter*, off Kimusa, in the South Seas. She was talking rapidly now, smiling, very excited. And then she jumped up and pointed to the butterflies, fluttering her brown hands. And in that moment I could not only see it all but feel it all. I felt for a moment as if I were Ephraim Franklin, standing off that island in the New Guineas, with the tropical heat and motionless sea and white sand and palms and the almost savage blue butterflies like those Ephraim had once caught for his father. Looking down at the ship and hearing her excited, almost childishly excited voice, I felt it all as a boy would feel it and was momentarily lost in wonder.

When I looked up again she was crying. And that was the oddest thing of all. I could understand her crying, but what I couldn't understand was the colour of her tears. They were white. And I couldn't get over that. I had somehow expected that they couldn't be anything but black. And while these white, so ordinary-looking gentle tears were rolling down her brown face the outside shop-bell rang.

I went and unbolted the shop door and it was the telegraph boy. I took in the telegram and came back into the room and put the envelope on the mantelpiece, not opening it. Then the girl and I went on playing with the ship, getting down more books, making more islands, sailing the ship dreamily among them, she laughing sometimes and then crying, overcome with joy at having found someone to make friends with at last.

Half an hour later my aunt came home. The mantelpiece was by that time empty of everything — all books and vases were islands — except the telegram. My aunt went straight to the telegram and opened it and read it. Then she stood utterly still.

And suddenly I knew it was about Ephraim. I did not know what to do or say. My aunt sank down into a chair and looked straight in front of her, saying "Ephraim" and holding the telegram in her shaking hands.

When the girl heard my aunt say 'Ephraim', she got suddenly very excited. "Ephraim yes?" she kept saying. "Hulloyes Ephraim, yes?"

"Ephraim's dead," my aunt said.

"Ephraim yes? Ephraim?" the girl said and she began laughing.

"Don't laugh!" my aunt said. "He's dead. Stop it! He's been drowned. The ship went down. Everybody's drowned."

The girl, not understanding, still so excited by the mention of Ephraim's name, kept on laughing.

My aunt began to cry, dryly, bitterly, without hope. She gave me the telegram. "Tell her, make her understand," she said. "Tell her."

For a moment I was so upset that I did not know what to do. Then after a moment or two I took hold of the ship. The girl watched me. I drove the ship across the hearthrug, tossing and pitching her terribly, giving her a great list to port, and then crashed her against the steel fender. I crashed her so hard, almost broadside on, that I cracked her planks on the starboard side and damaged her hull. When she heeled over I left her there and made great sea noises, washing the sea over her with my hands. Then suddenly I stopped and I just said "Ephraim, Ephraim," and shook my head and let my hands fall by my side. Then the girl understood. She just stood still too and began to cry again with the white, gentle ordinary-looking tears that were such a shock to me.

It is almost twenty-five years since all this happened. In six months the girl caught a chill and got pneumonia and died, and three months later my aunt died too. The shop is no longer there, and the ship, which my aunt gave me and which as I grew older I took less and less care of, has gone too.

But what I wanted to emphasize was this: that nothing can change the fact that for one afternoon I knew what it was like to be Ephraim Franklin, first mate and later master of *The Mary Porter*, and sail the seas in that ship, and anchor off the little island of Kimusa in the South Seas, and fall in love with a coloured girl.

Perhaps We Shall
Meet Again . . .

IT was no use, no use any longer. She must begin to eat less, much less; starve herself, cut out everything. It could not go on like this: public dinner after public dinner, company luncheons, lavish food, eating till she could not breathe, eating for the sake of eating. She must be firm, put a stop to it, now, at once, before the summer got too hot, before Victor got to be the director of any more companies. Two hundred and thirteen pounds. She saw the hands of the bathroom weight-clock revolve again, in imagination, and rest at that awful figure. She felt like weeping. It was something terrible. No woman could bear it. And so she had made up her mind. She was going to starve herself, and see what that would do.

She bounced and dumped along the edge of the lake, in the park, like a distended silk balloon, her feet still quite neat, her ankles incongruously bony still, so that it appeared as if she wore false legs. Her mind whispered and panted its little humiliations in small gas-escapes of misery.

On the edge of the lake, on the already hot grey concrete, small children were crumbling bread and saffron-yellow buns for the ducks. Mrs. Victor was revolted. Food, always food, eating, didn't the world do anything else? Gulls planed over and clawed the air, to swoop down and up and snatch the thrown bread before it reached the water. Their dismal crying greed set Mrs. Victor's nerves on edge like wire scratching on glass. She bumped and panted past, out of range of gulls and children and the revolting sight of bread thrown and snatched.

She sat down on one of the green public seats. There was another thing. Now it had got so that she couldn't sit on one of the twopenny chairs. They were made only, it seemed, for normal people, the slim and elegant. She remembered the days when she had been slim and elegant: straight as a line-prop, hardly fat enough in fact, her body its own corset.

Like the young woman on the seat. Just like her. Scarcely enough flesh, if anything. Mrs. Victor looked at the young woman who, in turn, was staring across the water: blonde, young, with shadow pointed cheeks and small scarlet buttonhole mouth closed tight up. Mrs. Victor, looking to see if she had any stockings on at all, saw the points of stitched ladders where the legs crossed. Stockings meant she had some sort of belt on. Well, that was just for decency. She didn't need support. It was a figure that had stepped straight out of advertisements.

Mrs. Victor looked down at her own squabbed-out thighs, like two vast aerated sausages, and felt like weeping. She could not bear it, and looked back at the girl.

Ask her if she diets. Somehow she looks as if she diets. That sort of thinness can't be natural. There's thinness and thinness. Somehow she looks as if she must diet.

Mrs. Victor hesitated to speak. She had seen the scorn, before now, in the faces of the young. She didn't want to speak and then have it thrown back in her face. Then she looked again at the girl. You could have blown her away with a breath. She had the ethereal lightness you saw spoken of in advertisements. There was nothing on her.

More children had appeared on the lake-edge, with more bread, so that the air was filled with a shrieking storm of gull-wings. Mrs. Victor said:

"Excuse me. I've been looking at your figure, and wondering — "

"Eh?" The girl, startled, turned her extraordinarily thin face. "I'm sorry. I can't hear for the birds."

For a moment the birds quietened. Mrs. Victor said:

"I hope you'll excuse my speaking to you. I've been looking at your figure. Wondering if you did anything special for it. If you dieted. You see how I am."

"No," the girl said. "I don't do anything special."

"Oh!"

Mrs. Victor, not knowing how to go on, smiled. The girl's profile looked as though it had been pared down by a knife.

"I've got so desperate now," she said, "that I'm thinking of seriously starving." It did not sound right. "Starving seriously," she said.

If she thinks I'm going to sit here, the girl thought, and listen, she's crazy. Not me. I'm going. I'll go straight away. She sat quite still. If I get up, she thought, I think I shall fall down.

"Really starving." Mrs. Victor went into an explanation of the word, moving slightly along the seat. "You know. Days without food."

"I know."

"I'm sick of food. Sick of it." Mrs. Victor began to explain who she was, how, being who she was, she had to attend dinners, functions, eating, always eating, eating until now, at last, she was utterly sick of eating. "Take last night. The dinner began at eight and we were still eating at half-past nine. Still eating!"

The girl sat trying to think of something to say. She could think of nothing but her suspender belt. It felt loose on her body.

It will fall off, she thought, if I move. I've altered the hooks once already. I shall have to alter them again.

"First there was some special sort of cheese, Norwegian or something, on rye-biscuit. As if we needed that. Then soup, *consommé* or *créme*, just the usual thing. Then fish. Fish I should have liked, but it was messed up with spaghetti and sauce and egg and I can't think what. All fattening things. And that's how it went on. Duck, pheasant, chicken — and I was so sick of them I tried venison. Have you ever eaten venison? My husband was having it and he said I should try it. I couldn't eat it. I can't explain what it tastes like — but queer, somehow. An acquired taste. You've never tried it?"

"No," the girl said, "I can't say I have."

"Don't."

I could eat an elephant, the girl thought. I could eat bacon rind. She sat thinking of bacon-rind. People didn't eat it. They cut it off, but if you did fry it, it jumped in the frying-pan like snakes.

"If you multiply that by hundreds you'll see what I have to go through in a year," Mrs. Victor said.

Multiply it by hundreds. Like snakes. Snakes lay eggs, hundreds of eggs. The girl remembered going, long ago, to the zoo, and then giving whole bananas to monkeys. It's not so bad, she thought. I had a banana yesterday. I made it last forty-three minutes. With luck I could make it last an hour.

"I've tried special baths. I've tried slimming creams and massage. I've tried everything," Mrs. Victor said. "It costs me a fortune." Children were beginning to come nearer, along the edge of the lake, drawing the gulls with them as though they were kites on invisible strings. Ducks scurried round in brown skirmishing flotillas, quarrelling, diving, tails up. "I've done everything, and this morning I went over fifteen. It's terrible. I used to be as thin as you."

It's no good, the girl thought, I've got to go down to the post office. If Harry sends the money I shall know it's all right. If he doesn't send it I know I'm done. Whatever happens, I've got to go down to the post office and see. I've got to be logical. I haven't a job.

I've got to be logical. During the war we used to eat locust beans. You never see them now. They said they had food value. We used to make them last a long time. That's what I want, something to last a long time.

"So I think there's nothing for it," Mrs. Victor said, "but to try simple starvation. I shall just starve and starve." She laughed a little. "After all it must be the oldest form of losing weight in the world."

The children had come very near, the gulls shrieking and wheeling above the flurry of ducks, white bread and yellow bunscraps flashing up in arcs against the bright sunshine.

"You see, it wears me out. Just sitting here now, I'm so hot I don't know what to do with myself. I'm all perspiration. I shall have to change everything when I get home."

A small child holding a round sugar-shining bun threw it into the water in one piece.

"It's so humiliating. You see, don't you? Your friends, people staring at you. When you've been thin, when you've had a nice figure. You see, don't you?"

"I see," the girl said.

"I envy you," Mrs. Victor said.

Again the girl thought, if I get up I shall fall down. She stirred slightly, feeling the emptiness of her stomach send out fainting waves of weakness. Her mind slipped into silliness. If A has two shillings between her and the workhouse and there's no letter at the post office how many bananas must A eat before A is dead?

On the edge of the lake a nurse stood on tip-toe and tried to regain the lost bun with the ferrule of a sunshade, regained it, and gave it back to the child. "Of course it's all right. Of course they'll eat it. They'll eat anything."

"I know my husband won't like it," Mrs. Victor said. "But I can't help it. He'll say think of my position and so on. But it's no use. I've got my own pride — I can't look at myself in the glass."

Now the small child had himself begun to eat the water-soaked bun, liking it. The nurse, grey-capped, swooped down on him like a gull herself, snatching it away, startling him to tears.

"Why does she make that child cry? I can't stand children crying," Mrs. Victor said. "It gets on my nerves. People think because you're fat and easy going you've got no nerves. My nerves are all on edge."

The crying of the small child against the crying of the gulls made wire-shrill discords. Nerves, the girl thought. Nerves. Somebody had said that to her. Nerve. She remembered, saw herself mooning slowly along the street, intentionless, her mind dead. You've got a nerve, a voice said. Beginners on the other side of the street. When you went to the cinema this was what happened. This, as you knew, was the thing that the heroine had to face, and yet it was never mentioned. It was the most terrible thing, and in the end, by some awful irony, it was the director who saved her both from it and from herself.

"That child," Mrs. Victor said. "I can't stand it. Why does she make it cry like that?"

The child, holding his breath, had gone from crimson to faint purple in the face, in the fury of his frustration. The waves of torturing sound beat against the great cushion of Mrs. Victor's body and shook her nerves. She got up.

"It's no use, I shall have to go."

At that moment the nurse snatched up the child, put him into a large white perambulator, snatched the bun from his hands and threw it into the lake again. In a moment, as the perambulator moved off, the screams of the child began to die away.

"Well, that's better," Mrs. Victor said. "Even so, I think I must go."

I must go too, the girl thought. But if I get up I shall faint.

"Good-bye," Mrs. Victor held out her hand. "Think of me starving." She held in her large moist hand the girl's thin one. "Perhaps we shall meet again."

"Good-bye," the girl said.

Mrs. Victor walked away along the edge of the lake. The girl sat staring at the water. Ducks and birds and light and bread revolved like a lucky wheel against the sun.

The Machine

EVERY evening, up at the farm, we saw the same men go past, out towards the villages, at the same time. They were coming home from the factories down in the valley: men escaping from the machine.

And though we got to know them well by sight, first the young chaps, racing hard, with flying mufflers, then the old stagers, the old tough shoe-finishers still wearing polish-blackened aprons, then the man with the black cork-leg and only one pedal to his bicycle, there was one we knew really well. His name was Simmons. We called him Waddo.

When Waddo went past we lifted hands from hoes or rakes, or even waved a cabbage that we might be cutting, and hailed him. "Way up!" we called.

"Waddo!" he shouted, and sailed on.

But three times a year, at hay-time, harvest and threshing, when we needed extra hands, he stopped to help us. He rode his pink-tyred semi-racing bike into the stack yard, unstrapped his dinner-basket, rolled up his sleeves and looked round at us, as we stood stacking corn or unloading hay, with a look of tolerant contempt. As though to say, "You poor miserable devils. Bin here since morning and all you done is stack up three ha'porth o' hay. Well, spit on me big toe, spit on it. If you ain't a bleedin' limit." It was the look of a giant for a degenerate collection of pitch-fork pygmies. Waddo himself stood five feet three.

But when he came into that yard we were transformed. He flung himself to work with an almost daemonic fury of strength. The muscles of his small arms were tight as clock-work springs under the white factory-blanched flesh. His little head, with thin wire-brush hair worn bald at the temples, was like a bullet that might have gone off at any moment with an explosive bang of enthusiasm or disgust. He worked swiftly, with the slight puffed swagger of a man of mountainous physique, incessantly talking, always comic, spitting mouthsful of patient disgust for us who worked so hard all day and did nothing. There was some extra volcanic force in Waddo, who never tired, never gave up, and was never beaten. Coming from the machines, he was like a machine himself. "Waddo," we'd say to him, "blowed if you don't go on wheels."

"I bleedin' well have to," he'd say, "don't I?" And we knew, with his five-mile ride to work and his five miles back, his eight-hour day holding boots to the jaws of a stitcher in the factory, his seven children, his readiness to mow with his own hands, in his spare time, every blade of grass and every standing acre of corn in the parish, how true it was. "I got a day's work to git through in half," he'd say. "Not like some folks."

"What you need on this place," he'd say at last, "is machinery."

In any discussion of the machine Waddo held us as it were at arm's length, in contempt. "Call yourself bleedin' farmers, and ain't got a machine on the place. No binder, no hay-turner, no root-cutter. No tater-riddler, no nothing. Blimey, spit on me big toe, spit on it. Ain't you up to date? Here you are scrattin' about like old hens scrattin' for daylight, when a couple o' machines'd bring you right bang-slap up with the times. Machines — that's what you want. Save yourself time and money. See! They do away with the men."

The machine was his god. It was exemplified in his racing bike, in the stitcher which he fed all day with boots like some omnivorous steel brute at the factory, in the threshing-drum we hired once every winter. Working so beautifully, swiftly and naturally with his own hands, he exalted the mechanism that could have cut out the element of man. It fed his devotion with the same daemonic energy as he worked, so that he preached at us with one hand on the futility of a machineless world and showed us, with the other, how incomparable and effective it could be. With the machinery of his two hands he swung a scythe with a masterly and precise beauty that no machine could ever have shown.

And at heart, I think, he knew it. He mowed very fast, as though carelessly, off-hand, apparently indifferent. He was often not so tall, by a foot, as the corn he cut. Head down, he had a certain air of detached dreaminess, as though the whole thing meant nothing to him at all.

Then, at the end of the swathe, he would turn and look back; and we would see, for a moment, the beauty of the work recaptured in his own eye, the small light of pleasure glinting out as though a bead of sweat had been caught in the pupil. He gazed, as we did, at the level alleys of stubble, short and straight as though the corn were sprouting up white again, the golden-white corn stalks shining as if sun-oiled, the sienna-gold sweep of ears and the straight wall of standing corn, and he must have known that he was a master hand.

But always in time, the obsession of the machine caught him up again. "How many acres of wheat you got here? Ten? Gonna take us a week to move it. Now with a binder — "

We would say something about expense.

"Expense! Spit on me big toe. You can't see for looking. Expense! You can save the bleedin' cost of the thing in a couple o' years. Save money, save men. Don't you see?"

Sometimes he would work on into the still August moonlight, tireless as a machine himself, mowing, whetting the scythe, dropping the scythe to fall flat on some escaping leveret, mowing again, still arguing, still abusing us, then biking off, at last, across the moon-dewed land with the energy of a man just beginning a cycle race.

"Don't you want a light?" we'd say to him.

"Light? Spit on me big toe, I s'll be home and in bed with the missus afore you can strike a match."

He abused and decried us all through harvest and hay-making. At threshing he got his reward. In the engine and drum he saw, at last, a sensible interpretation of life: a complicated system of power and steam, a miracle, a single unit doing the work of scores of men. "Some sense," he'd say, "at last."

He took a day off from the factory, then, to help us, arriving at six in the morning, and we saw then that we had never seen him except as a tired man. He skidded into the yard at full speed, bounced off his bicycle, seized his pitch-fork as though ready to lift a complete corn-stack with one finger. He argued vociferously, held us at the usual arm's length of contempt, laughed and joked and worked as always with the same casual and yet explosive and masterly rhythm. Working high up in the drum, on the edge of a maelstrom, he bawled down to us below with gigantic accents, though nobody could hear, feeding sheaves to the drum with the pleasure of a man feeding a favourite beast.

We threshed, one year, in November. The wind came down on us from the north-east, with intermittent bites of ice-rain, across bare land. The power of the wind roaring under the drum spouted up a terrific blast of chaff, all day long, that was like hail on the naked eyes. Above, chaff and chaff-dust were winnowed from the cracks of the drum in fierce little clouds, as though she were spitting ice vapour. Higher still, on the roof of the drum, the men caught by the full force of wind and up-blown chaff and wind-blasted straw worked all day half-blinded.

Waddo was on the drum. Exhilarant in that terrific wind, he worked as though the wind shot him new energy. He bawled down at us with a mouth that, against the roar of drum and engine and wind, was quite soundless. But we understood, we felt the words in his expression of contemptuous triumph. "See? Didn't I tell you? Spit on me toe — didn't I tell you what a machine could save you?"

That day the rats began to run out of the first stack about eleven o'clock. We pursued and hemmed and cornered them, smashing them to lumps of grey-red jelly in the wind-littered straw. From above Waddo looked down on us like a director of operations, yelling and waving his fork.

As he stood there, jack-in-the-boxing, gesticulating, laughing, a rat leapt out of a sheaf he was lifting. We saw his own leap of energetic excitement and knew the words he yelled by long habit and the shaping of his lips:

"Spit on me big toe, spit on it! Waddo! Spit on me — "

We saw him slip. We knew how the iron-shod boots must have slid on the loose kernels of polished grain, on the straw-smoothed roof of the drum. He lifted a wild hand and he yelled and shouted. The engine-man threw on the brakes and we heard the shriek and moan of stopped machinery.

"Waddo!" we yelled, "Waddo. For Christ's sake! Waddo!"

There was no answer; and in a world that stood still we knew that the machine had claimed him.

I Am Not Myself

IT was summer when the Arnoldsons first asked me to go and stay with them. I could not go. I did not go until the following winter, on January 5th. It was bitterly cold that day, with thin drifts of snow whipped up from the ground like fierce white sandstorms, and there was snow on the ground almost every day until I left, four days later.

The Arnoldsons lived about seven miles from the nearest town. The house is quite ordinary: plain red brick, double-fronted, with large bay-windows and a large brass-knockered front door and a spotless white doorstep. It is the colour of a new flower-pot and at the back in the garden there is a long pergola of bay-trees which is like a tunnel leading to nowhere.

Before that day in January I did not know any of the Arnoldsons except Laurence. We were at school together but we had not seen each other for fifteen years. He was an architect and

146

I had written a letter to a paper about country architecture and he had seen it and that was how the invitation to stay with them had come about. Laurence Arnoldson is a man of medium height with straight dark hair brushed back. He wears plain ascetic looking gold spectacles and is a man of meticulous habits; always paring his finger-nails, polishing his glasses, splitting life into millimetres. His craze for exactitude and his contempt for people who have no time for it have made him a prig. He holds his head very high and you can see him looking down his nose at the world. The best thing about him are his eyes: they are weak but they are a deep, rather strange shade of brown. There is something remote about them.

Laurence met me at the station that day in a fairly old but carefully kept Morris-Oxford, a four-seater. His father was with him. He sat in the front seat, huddled in a black rug, with a large shaggy grey scarf muffled round his head. The scarf covered almost all of his face except his eyes. As Laurence introduced me I saw that his father's eyes had exactly the same deep remote brownness as the son's. It was snowing a little at the time and Laurence had left the windscreen wiper working and I could see the man's eyes mechanically following its pendulum motions. They slid to and fro like two brown ball-bearings moving in grey oil, fascinated by the clear glass arc made by the wiper in the furred snow.

Laurence's father did not speak to me and neither he nor Laurence exchanged a word as we drove slowly out into the frozen country. Their silence depressed me. I felt it had something to do with myself. Now and then I made a remark and once, about half a mile from the house, we passed a pond frozen over and I said something about skating and Laurence said:

"Oh! Yes. That's the pond where my sister saw a fox walk across the ice yesterday."

The Arnoldson's house stands on what was formerly a private estate and there is a private gravel road half a mile long leading up to it through fenceless fields that are planted with groups of elm and lime.

There is no Mrs. Arnoldson. She has been dead for thirteen years, and the house has been run for all that time by her sister, aunt Wilcox. It was aunt Wilcox who met us at the front door that afternoon, a dumpy woman with white hair scraped back sharply from her soap-polished face. She came out of the house briskly, shook hands with me without waiting to be introduced and then helped Mr. Arnoldson out of the car. I thought at first he had been ill, but then as he stood upright I could see that there was nothing wrong with him and that he was really a big and rather powerful man. His hands were very large-boned and his head, hugely swathed in the great scarf, had a kind of ill-balanced power about it. It swayed slightly to and fro as he walked, as though it were loose on the spine. He did not speak to me.

Aunt Wilcox spoke with a strong Yorkshire accent. The Arnoldsons themselves are Yorkshire people and the house is furnished in Yorkshire fashion: a rocking-chair in every room, big dressers, patchwork cushions, heavy pink-and-gold tea services. In the large drawing-room the curtains are of some claret-coloured woollen material, with plush bobbles, and they hang from great mahogany rods by mahogany rings that are like the rings on a hoop-la. On the mantelpiece stand two large china dogs, spaniels, black and white. They face each other and they appear to be looking at the same thing. They are extraordinarily lifelike.

I had been upstairs to unpack my things and had come down again and was looking at these dogs when Laurence came in to say that tea was ready. We went across the hall into the opposite room. It was about four o'clock and the white reflected light of the fallen snow was prolonging by a few minutes the fall of darkness. We sat down to tea in this strange snow-twilight, aunt Wilcox and Mr. Arnoldson opposite each other at the ends of the table, Laurence and I opposite, I myself opposite the window. The room was the exact reflection of the other. At the windows were the same sort of heavy woollen-bobbled curtains and on the mantelpiece stood what might have been the same pair of china spaniels watching with extraordinary lifelike fixedness some invisible object between them.

We sat there eating and drinking, without saying much. Aunt Wilcox poured tea from a huge electroplated pot that might have held a gallon. The cups were like pink and gold basins.

I drink my tea very hot and suddenly, as aunt Wilcox was taking my empty cup, I saw someone coming up the road towards the house. I knew at once, somehow, that it was Laurence's sister. She was wearing a big brown coat, but no hat. Every now and then she stepped off the road on to the grass and wandered off, as though looking for something. She was like someone playing follow-my-leader with herself. Once she wandered farther off than usual and in the half-darkness I lost her for a moment. Then I saw her again. She was running. She was running quite fast and all at once she fell down on her knees in the snow and then ran on again. She was still running when she came to the house.

Two minutes later she came in. Her knees and the fringe of her coat were covered with snow where she had fallen down and there was a small salt-sprinkling of snow on her hair. She was about twenty-three, but she looked much younger, and I shall never forget how she came in, out of breath, to look at us with the same remote brown eyes as Laurence's, intensely excited, with a stare that had nothing to do with earth at all.

"I saw him again," she said.

For a moment no one spoke. Then Laurence said:

"Who? The fox?"

"Yes. I saw him run over the pond again and then I chased him up through the park and then just as I got near the house I lost him."

No one spoke a word.

* * *

That evening, after supper, she told me more about the fox. She described him: how bright he was and how good-coloured and how it was only in snowy or frosty weather that she saw him, and as she described him I saw him, bright, quiet, his back feet slipping from under him a little as he sloped across the ice on the small pond. I saw him as she saw him, as she wanted me to see him.

She told me about the fox in two or three minutes. She talked rather quickly, but all her impressions were in reality created with her eyes; the images of fox and snow and frozen pond were thrown up in them with untarnishable clarity. Unlike a great many people she looked straight at me while talking. Her eyes were full of great candour. They looked straight forward, with natural ardour. You felt that they could never look sideways. They had in them an unblemished honesty that was very beautiful and also very convincing, but also, in some way, empty.

For those two or three minutes we were alone. We had all had supper and we were going to play cribbage. Laurence had gone into his room to finish a letter and aunt Wilcox was in the kitchen. Mr. Arnoldson had gone upstairs to find a new pack of cards.

"I'd like to come out in the morning," I said, "and see this fox."

She did not say anything.

In a little while first Laurence, and then Mr. Arnoldson and then aunt Wilcox came back, and we made arrangements to play. Cribbage was the only card game all of us knew and we decided to play in two pairs, for a shilling a horse, man out scoring. We cut the cards, ace high, lowest out, and aunt Wilcox said:

"It's you, Christiana. Mind now, no edging."

The girl had cut a two of hearts, and I realized suddenly that it was the first time I had heard her name.

Aunt Wilcox and I played together. We were both rather quick, downright players, quick to sense a hand. We always had the pips counted before we put them on the table. This was not the Arnoldson way. Deliberation, to me an increasingly irritating deliberation, marked everything Laurence and his father did. They weighed up their hands guardedly and put on poker expressions, giving nothing away. Just as the girl spoke with her eyes, they played with their eyes. Between the counting of the hands they did not speak a word.

The game was a near thing and it

154

looked, for a moment, as if aunt Wilcox and I might die in the hole, but we got home and I noticed aunt Wilcox pocketing the shilling. The Arnoldsons were not at all satisfied, and Laurence went over the last hand again, architect fashion, checking up, before giving in.

Mr. Arnoldson looked at Christiana. I forgot to say that he had a large grey sheep-dog moustache. The expression of his mouth was thus hidden. The whole expression of his face was compressed into his eyes. They shone very brightly, with a rather queer glassy look of excitement.

For the second game aunt Wilcox dropped out and Christiana took her place, playing with me. She was the quickest player I had ever seen. Every player gets now and then a hand he cannot make up his mind about, but that never happened to her. She played by instinct, second sight. She hardly looked at the cards. She kept her eyes on me. Yet she made up her mind before we began. I felt that, in some miraculous way, she could see through the cards.

All through the game she sat with her eyes on me. This constant but completely passionless stare had me beaten. It was hypnotic, so that whenever I looked away from her I was conscious of being drawn back. At first I thought it was deliberate, that she was simply trying hard to attract me. Then I got into the way of accepting her stare, of returning it. But where there should have been some response, there was only an unchanged anonymity, a beautiful brown wateriness filled with a remote, quietly hypnotic strength. I saw her as one of those composite pictures of two people. Two personalities are fused and there remains no personality, only some discomforting anonymity that fascinates.

During the game the tension between Christiana and her father increased. She was constantly one leap ahead of us all. She knew; we guessed. She had good cards, twice a hand of twenty-four. All the time I could see Mr. Arnoldson fidgeting, his eyes generating new phases of resentment.

Aunt Wilcox seemed to understand this. The Christmas decorations were still hanging up in the house, sprays of holly, withering now, stuck up behind the pictures, and a wand or two of box and fir. Suddenly aunt Wilcox said:

"Twelfth day to-morrow. We mustn't forget the decorations."

"Pancakes," Christiana said.

"Fifteen two and a pair's four and three's seven," I said. "Pancakes?"

"A north-country custom," aunt Wilcox said. "You fry the pancakes with a fire of the evergreens."

"I think," Laurence said, "I have a pair." He slowly laid out his cards. "Mind you don't set the chimney on fire."

Suddenly Christiana's hand was on the table. She counted it like a parrot saying something by heart. She had three sixes and a nine and a three was up and she rattled it off, running the words together, making eighteen. Eighteen was quite right, but Mr. Arnoldson sprang to his feet, as though he had not heard it.

"Nineteen, nineteen, you can't score nineteen!" he shouted. "It's not possible in crib!"

"I said eighteen!"

"Eighteen is right," I began.

"She said nineteen. I heard her. I

distinctly heard her. You think I don't know her voice?"

"Eighteen!" she said.

"You said nineteen and now you're lying on top of it!"

He was on his feet, shouting at her, grey with anger. Suddenly he began to shake violently and I knew he had lost control. He turned round and picked up the heavy mahogany Yorkshire chair he had been sitting in and swung it about, over his head. Aunt Wilcox got hold of Christiana and half pushed, half dragged her out of the room, and I automatically went after her, shouting after her as she ran upstairs in the darkness.

When I went back into the room, a moment later, Mr. Arnoldson was lying on the hearth-rug, on his back, in a fit. The chair was lying smashed on the table where he had brought it down. He was clenching in his hands some bits of withered holly he had torn down from one of the pictures. His hands were bleeding and it was a long time before we could get them open again.

★ ★ ★

The next morning Laurence, aunt Wilcox, Christiana and I sat down to a large and healthy breakfast, plates of porridge, lumps of rather fat beef-steak with fried mashed potatoes and eggs, thick toast and very strong marmalade, with the usual basins of tea. It was all very solid, very real. Unlike the behaviour of Mr. Arnoldson on the previous night it was something you could get your hands on and understand. Mr. Arnoldson did not appear at breakfast and no one said anything about him.

During breakfast Laurence read his letters and said he had a couple of hours' work to do and would I mind amusing myself? In the afternoon we could go and look at some houses; there were one or two good stone mansions in the neighbourhood. It was still bitterly cold that morning, but there had been no more snow. The snow of yesterday had been driven, like white sand, into thin drifts, leaving exposed black islands of ice.

I decided to go for a walk, and after breakfast I asked Christiana to come with me. "We could look for the fox," I said.

Except for refusing, she did not say much. She was going to help aunt Wilcox. About the fox she was very evasive. It might not have existed. She might not have seen it.

"I'll have a look for it myself," I said.

She looked at me emptily, not speaking. Her eyes had lost completely the natural ardour and candour, both very child-like, which had infused the picture of the fox with reality and which had made me believe in both it and her. At that moment she could not have made me believe in anything.

I got my overcoat and gloves and went out. It was an east wind, steady, bitter, the sky a dull iron colour, without sun. In the fields the grass had been driven flat by wind. The earth was like rock. In a scoop of the land a small stream flowed down between squat clumps of alder, catkins wind-frozen, cat-ice jagging out like frosted-glass from the fringe of frost-burnt rushes on both banks. Farther on a flock of pigeons clapped up from a field of white kale, clattering wings on steel leaves, spiralling up, gathering,

160

separating again like broken bits of the dead sky.

I went on until I found the pond. I knew it at once because, a field away, I could see the road, and because of what Christiana had said about it. She had described the black sloe bushes barricading one side, the speared army of dead rushes, and a broken-down, now half — submerged cattle trough on which the fox, she said, had leapt and sat and stared at her. The pond was covered with ice and the ice in turn with the fine salt snow swept in a succession of smooth drifts across it.

I stood and looked at the pond. Then I walked round it. At the opposite point, by the cattle-trough, I stood and looked at it again. On the cattle-trough the light snow crusts were unbroken, and on two sides of it, away from the water, snow had drifted in long arcs, rippled and firm as lard. On the trough and in the snow drifted round it and all across the pond there were no marks of any fox at all.

* * *

When I got back to the house, about twelve, aunt Wilcox and Christiana were taking down the decorations. Most of the evergreens had been hung up in the hall, holly behind the pictures, sheaves of yew tied to the newel-posts of the polished pine staircase, and a very dry spray of mistletoe hung from the big brass oil-lamp. Aunt Wilcox and Christiana were putting the evergreens into a zinc bath-tin.

"You're just in time," Christiana said.

"Last come must last kiss," aunt Wilcox said.

"And what does that mean?" I said.

"You've got to kiss us both."

Laughing, aunt Wilcox stood under the mistletoe and I kissed her. Her lips were solid and sinewy, like beefsteak, and lukewarm wet. As she clasped me round the waist I felt her coopered, with stays, like a barrel. Then Christiana stood under the mistletoe and I kissed her. Just before I kissed her she looked at me for a moment. Her eyes had the same remote anonymity as on the previous day, the same tranquil but disturbing candour. As I kissed her she was quite still, without fuss. Kissing her was like kissing someone who was not there. It was a relationship of ghosts. For one moment I felt I was not there myself. The recollection of this unreal lightness of touch was something I carried about with me for the rest of the day.

That afternoon Laurence and I went for a walk. I asked after his father and he said he was better, but resting. We talked about him for a short time. He told me how he had begun as a pit-boy in a Yorkshire colliery, but had worked himself up, and had later become a schoolmaster. Then the war broke out and he felt suddenly that he was wasted in the classroom and had gone back to the pit, to become under-manager. After about six months there was a disaster in the pit, an explosion that had brought down a vast roof-fall, entombing thirty-five men. Arnoldson went down for rescue work. For two days he could hear the voices of the entombed men quite clearly, then for a whole day he could hear them intermittently, then they ceased. But though they ceased Arnoldson fancied all the time he could still hear them, the voices of the dead, of men he had known, screaming or whispering in his mind more sharply than in life. He went on hearing these voices for weeks, the voices of people who were not there, until they broke him down. Christiana had been born about a year later.

Laurence spoke of his father with a slight impatience. He spoke as though, occupied himself with concrete things, the small matter of voices disturbing the spirit of another man had no material importance for him. It was clear that he did not believe in voices. From the subject of his father we went on to the subject of himself. I walked with head slightly down, mouth set against the wind, saying yes and no, not really listening, my thoughts in reality a long way behind me, like a kite on a string.

When we got back to the house, about four o'clock, I noticed a curious thing as we went past the dining-room. The door of the room was open and I could see that one of the china spaniel dogs was missing from the mantelpiece. At the time I did not take much notice of this. I went upstairs to wash my hands and came down and went into the drawing-room. Christiana sat reading by the fire, but for about half a minute I did not look at her. One of the china dogs was missing from the mantelpiece.

It was only about ten seconds after this that I heard Laurence coming downstairs. His way of coming downstairs was unmistakable. I heard his feet clipping the edges of the stairs with the precision of an engine firing in all its cylinders: the assured descent of a man who knew he could never fall down.

As he came down into the hall Christiana suddenly went to the door and said in a loud voice:

"Tea's ready. You're just right."

We went straight into the dining-room. Christiana was last. She shut the door of the drawing-room after her. On the mantelpiece of the dining-room the two china dogs sat facing each other.

All through tea I sat looking at Christiana. She sat looking at me, but without any relationship between the eyes and the mind. Her eyes rested on me with a stare of beautiful emptiness. It might have been a stare of wonder or distrust or adoration or appeal: I could not tell. There was no way of telling. For the first time I saw some connection between this expressive vacancy and the voices that Mr. Arnoldson had heard in his mind. Sitting still, eyes dead straight but not conscious, she looked as though she also were listening to some voices very far away.

Just as we were finishing tea, aunt Wilcox said to me: "I hope you didn't get cold this afternoon. You look a bit peaked."

"I'm all right," I said. "But I never really got my feet warm."

"Why don't you go and put on your slippers?" Christiana said.

"I'd like to," I said.

So I went upstairs to put on my slippers, while Laurence went to write his evening letters, and aunt Wilcox and Christiana cleared the table. It was Sunday and aunt Wilcox was going to chapel.

I came downstairs again in less than five minutes. Christiana was sitting by the fire in the drawing-room. The two china dogs sat on the mantelpiece. I looked at

166

the dogs, then at Christiana, with double deliberation. She must have seen I was trying to reason it out, that perhaps I had reasoned it out, but she gave no sign.

I sat down and we began to talk. It was warm; the small reading lamp imprisoned us, as it were, in a small world of light, the rest of the room an outer darkness. I tried to get her to talk of the fox. There was no response. It was like pressing the buttons of a dead door-bell. Once I said something about her father. "He's asleep," she said. That was all. We went on to talk of various odd things. She lay back in the chair, facing the light, looking quietly at me. I fixed my eyes on hers. I had a feeling, very strong after a few minutes, that she wanted me to touch her. All at once she asked me had I ever been abroad? I said: "Yes, to France once, and Holland once. That's all. Holland is lovely." She did not say anything at once. She looked slowly away from me, down at the floor, as though she could see something in the darkness beyond the ring of light. Suddenly she said: "I've been to Mexico, that's all." I asked her for how long. She looked up at me. Without answering my question she began to tell me about Mexico. She told me about it as she had told me about the fox, speaking rather quickly, telling me where she had been, reciting the beautiful names of the places, talking about the food, the colour, the women's dresses. I had a feeling of travelling through a country in a train, in a hurry, getting the vivid transient panoramic effect of fields and villages, sun and trees, of faces and hands suddenly uplifted. She described everything quickly, her voice certain and regular, like a train passing over metals. She described an episode about Indians, how she had gone up into the mountains, to a small town where there was a market, where thin emaciated Indians came down to sell things, squatting close together on the ground in the cold, with phlegmatic and degenerate eyes downcast. There a woman had tried to sell her a few wizened tomatoes, holding them out with blue old veined hands, not speaking, simply holding the tomatoes out to her. Then suddenly, because the girl would not have them, the woman had squeezed one of them in a rage until seeds and juice ran out like reddish-yellow blood oozing out of the fissure between her frozen knuckles. As the girl told it, I felt rather than saw it. I felt the bitter coldness of the little town cut by mountain winds and the half-frozen juice of the tomato running down my own hands.

She went on talking, with intervals, for about an hour. After a time, some time after she had told me about the Indian woman, I had again the feeling that she wanted me to touch her. Her hands were spread out on her lap. I watched the light on them. I could see the slight upheaval of the white fingers, regular and intense, as she breathed, and this small but intense motion radiated a feeling of inordinate and almost fearful strength. The effect on me was as though I were looking down into very deep, not quite still water: an effect slightly hypnotic, slightly pleasurable, quietly governed by fear. I felt afraid to take my eyes away from her and I felt, after a time, that she did not want me to take them away.

After a time I did something else I

knew she wanted me to do. I went and sat by her, in the same chair. I put my arms round her, not speaking a word. As I held her I could feel her listening. Perhaps she is listening, I thought, for someone to come. She did not speak. I could feel her fingers, outspread, clutching my back, as though she were falling into space. After a time she spoke.

"What did you say?" she said. I sat silent. "What did you say?" she said. "I thought I heard you say something."

"No," I said, "I didn't speak."

"Perhaps it was someone else?" she said.

I sat still. I did not say anything. Her breathing was slightly deeper. All the time I could feel her listening, as though waiting for the echo of some minute explosion on the other side of the earth.

"Don't you ever think you hear the voices of people who are not here?"

"Everybody does that," I said.

"I mean you."

"Sometimes."

"Often?"

"Not often."

The small reading lamp stood on a table between the chair and the fireplace. I felt her stretch out her hand towards it. About us, for one moment the house seemed dead still. She put out the light. I heard the small click of the switch freeing us, as it were, from the restriction of light. She put her hands on my face, held it. I remember wondering suddenly what sort of night it was, if it were starlight, whether there was snow.

"Can you see me?" she said.

"No."

"I can see you."

I felt her withdraw herself very slightly from me. Then I knew why she could see me. I was sitting facing the window and through the slits of the dark curtains I could see blurred snow-white chinks of moonlight.

★ ★ ★

We did not have supper, that night, until nine o'clock. We had Yorkshire ham and pork pie, cold apple tart with red cheese, mincepies and cheesecakes, with large basins of strong tea. Aunt Wilcox had pickles and towards the end of the meal we pulled half a dozen crackers that had been left over from Christmas. Out of her cracker Christiana had a tall white paper hat in the twelfth-century style, pointed, like a cone. As she put it on I got an instant impression that the dark brown eyes, under the white cap, looked darker than ever, and that they were slightly strange, not quite real, and for the first time it hurt me to look at them.

This impression continued until the following day. The moonlight was very strong nearly all night and I did not sleep well. All through the next morning I wanted to be alone with Christiana, but the chance did not seem to come. Mr. Arnoldson came downstairs and sat all day in front of the drawing-room fire, wrapped in rugs, so that the drawing-room was never empty. The two china dogs sat on the mantelpiece there and were not, as on the previous day, changed at all. Once I heard the voices of aunt Wilcox and Christiana coming from the kitchen. They were talking about the dogs. "It's in my room," Christiana said. "I've stuck it with seccotine." I sat most of that morning in Laurence's study, reading. He went in mostly for technical books and towards the end of the morning I got bored and asked him if he had any books of travel. He said there were a few in his bedroom. I went up to his room and there, on his chest of drawers, I found a book on Mexico. I took it downstairs and in five minutes I was reading the episode about the tomato and the Indian woman in the little cold mountain town.

In the night there had been another fall of snow, but it was a little warmer. The sun was very brilliant on the snow and out of Laurence's study window I could see, high up, peewits flashing like semaphores, white and dark against the very blue winter sky. I felt I had to get out.

I went out and walked across the fields, in the snow, past the brook and over towards the pond. The white of the snow was dazzling and I felt a slightly dazed effect, the light too sharp for my eyes. Along by the brook the snow was beginning to melt a little on the branches of the alders, bringing down showers of bright ice rain. I could see everywhere where rabbits had loped about in the early morning snow and there were many prints of moorhens, but there was nothing that looked at all like the mark of a fox.

The snow had covered everything of the pond and the surface was smoother than water. I stood and looked at it for a moment and then went on. A little farther on I picked up the brook again and I did not come back for half an hour.

Coming back I saw Christiana. I could see where she had walked in the snow. She had walked round the pond and now she was about half a field away, going back towards the house. I called and she turned and waited for me, standing against the sun. She stood with her arms folded, her big coat lapped heavily over her. Her face was white with the strong upward reflection of snow.

We walked on together. She walked with her arms continually folded. "Have you seen the fox?" I said.

She did not answer. I knew I did not

expect her to answer. Farther on we had to cross the brook by a small wooden bridge. On the bridge I stopped her, holding her coat. I put my arms round her and held her for a moment. Holding her, I could feel, then, why she walked with her arms folded. She had something under her coat. She kissed me without speaking. All the time I could feel her holding some object under her coat, as hard as stone.

We stood there, above the sun-shining water, slightly dazzled by the world of snow, for about five minutes, and I kissed her again. She was acquiescent, but it was an acquiescence that was stronger, by a long way, than all the strange remote activity of her spirit had ever been. It was normal. I felt for the first time that she was there, very young, very sweet, very real, perhaps a little frightened. Up to that time we had said nothing at all about affection. I had not thought of it. Now I wanted her. It seemed very natural, an inevitable part of things.

"You like me, don't you?" I said. It was all I could think of saying.

"Yes," she said.

"Very much?"

"Very much."

She smiled very quietly. I did not know what to do except to smile back. We walked on. Out in the open snow I stopped and, before she could do or say anything, kissed her again.

"Someone will see us."

"I don't care," I said.

I was very happy. At that moment, out in the snow, walking away from the sun, watching our two blue shadows climbing before us up the slight slope to the house, I had no doubts about her. Half an hour before I had wanted to tell her that I knew there was no fox, that she had never been to Mexico, that all that she had told me was an imposture. Now it did not seem to matter. And the voices? They did not seem to matter either. Many people hear the voices of people who are not there, who have never been there. There is nothing strange in that.

I was worried only by one thing: what she was carrying under her coat. Then, when we went in for lunch I knew, for certain, that it was the china dog. And that night I knew why it was.

Mr. Arnoldson went to bed very early that night, about half-past seven, and aunt Wilcox went upstairs with him, to see that he was all right. Laurence had gone down to the post office and I was sitting in the drawing-room, reading the morning paper. From the dining-room, suddenly, I could hear voices.

They went on for five minutes and I could not understand it. At last I got up and opened the drawing-room door. Across the hall the dining-room door was open a little and Christiana was sitting at the dining table, talking to a china dog.

"The fox," she was saying, "the fox!"

I stood looking. She was jabbering quite fast to the dog, strangely excited, her fingers tense.

"Christiana," I said.

She did not hear me.

"Christiana."

She got the dog by the neck and ran it across the mahogany table, towards a glass fruit dish, in crazy pursuit of something, jabbering, laughing a little, until I could see that the dog had the fox by the neck and that they were tearing each other to bits in the snow.

I saw it quite clearly for a moment, like a vision: the mahogany changed to snow, the fruit dish to fox, the china dog to a dog in reality, and in that moment, for the first time, I felt a little mad myself.

I went away on the following afternoon. Laurence drove me to the station. Nothing much happened. It was snowing fast and Christiana did not come outside to see us off. She stood at the window of the drawing-room, staring out. Except that her face was white with the reflection of the snow, she looked quite normal, quite herself. No one would have noticed anything. But as we drove away I saw her, for one second, as someone imprisoned, cut off from the world, shut away.

We had not much time for the train and Laurence drove rather fast. "You look a bit queer," he said at the station. "Are you all right?"

"Yes," I said.

"Are you sure? Let me carry your bag. You don't look quite yourself."

I could not speak. No, I thought, I am not myself.

The Flying Goat

WHAT? the man in the saloon said to me, you never heard of Jethro Watkins's flying goat? Well, there was a chap in this town, once, who made himself a pair of straw wings; strapped them on his shoulders, jumped off the top of a house and broke his neck. Then there was another chap who made himself a bicycle with wings; he called it a flycycle, and he flycycled over the top of a precipice and broke his neck. But Jethro Watkins had a flying goat. I don't mean a goat that flew with wings. I mean a goat that flew without wings. And when I say flew I mean flew. I don't mean it jumped over some three-foot railings and flew by mistake. It flew regularly. It flew all over England. Surely, he said, you must have heard of Jethro Watkins's flying goat?

"No," I told him, "I never heard of it."

Well, that's funny, he said. You mean you never heard about the time it flew off the tower at Blackpool?

"No," I told him, "I can't say I did."

No? he said. Then you must have heard about the time it flew fifteen times round the tent in Wombwell's circus?

"No," I told him, "I can't say I heard about that either."

I don't know, he said, I'm sure. It's funny. Nowadays nobody seems to have heard about anything.

"Well, who was this Jethro Watkins?" I said.

Well, in the first place he was a very religious chap, he said. He was in the Salvation Army. Used to play the euphonium. And then he was very fat — weighed fifteen, perhaps sixteen stone — and by trade he was a thatcher, — you know what I mean, he thatched roofs and stacks. Always up on a ladder, catching every bit of wind. Well, Jethro told me how what with being a euphonium player and a thatcher and always being concerned with wind one way or another he began to study wind. Up there, on his ladder, he used to see what wind could do — toss birds about, toss whole armsful of straw about, almost lift a roof off before he got it pegged down. You know how powerful a big wind is — blows trees down, even blows houses down. Well, Jethro had been studying all that years before he got this idea of a flying goat.

"And how," I said, "did he get this idea of a flying goat?"

Like all big ideas, he said. By accident. Just like that. All of a pop. He saw some posters about a menagerie and one of the items was a flying ape and Jethro went to see it. Well, there wasn't much in it. Just a big grey-looking ape that did a big trapeze jump and they called it flying. Well, Jethro thought it was a swindle. He went home in disgust and he went and stood in his back-yard and looked at his goats. Did I tell you he kept goats? No? Well, he'd kept goats for years — bred and raised them. One of the things that made him such a strong, big fat man was goats' milk. He'd drunk it twice a day for years. And suddenly he had this big idea — a flying goat. If a monkey could fly, why not a goat? And if a man could make money out of a flying ape, why couldn't he make money out of a flying goat? The thatching trade had been going down steadily for years, and just about that time it had got down almost to a standstill. So this idea of a flying goat was a godsend. Providence. According to Jethro's idea it was God stretching down a helping hand.

"Now you're going to tell me," I said, "that he taught the goat to fly until it could fly well enough to fly round a circus?"

Well, no, he said. That's what he tried to do. But it didn't come off. He got one of his goats and started to train it in the back-yard — you know, put it first on a beer-barrel and made it jump off, then on two beer-barrels, and then on a painter's trestle about fifteen feet high. But it was no good. He could see he'd made a mistake.

"Now don't tell me," I said, "that this is all a mistake?"

No, he said. The idea of training a goat to fly was a mistake, that's all. Jethro could see that. No, what he did do was to breed a goat that could fly — you see how I mean, a sort of miracle. Jethro was a very religious chap — Salvation Army meetings, playing in the band, believing in the Bible and all that. And suddenly that's how he saw it. I want a flying goat, he thought, and if I want it badly enough and ask God then God will perform a miracle and see that I get it. If God doesn't approve I shan't get it and then I shall know it was wrong to ask for it. So he mated two of his goats and prayed for a miracle to happen and waited. He prayed twice a day, morning and night, for a kid that could fly. He knew all about miracles. If five thousand people could be fed with two loaves and five small fishes, or if somebody could raise a boy from the dead or if a sick man could pick up his bed and walk then why shouldn't an ordinary chap like himself get a simple thing like a goat that could fly? Ask yourself. It was reasonable.

"And now you're going to tell me," I said, "that in due course the kid was born and it could fly from birth like a bird?"

It was, he said, and it could. The second day of its life it began to jump up in the air. Like a lamb, only higher. Then the third it jumped higher still.

The fourth day it flew over its mother. Flew, not jumped. Then by the end of the week it was flying over fences. It flew over a row of kidney-beans in Jethro's garden. Inside a month it could fly over a haystack. It was a lovely white colour, and Jethro told me it was so light that you could hold it in your hand like a ball of cotton wool.

"Then what?" I said.

Well, Jethro had another idea. It was through the Grace of God that I got the goat, he thought. The right thing to do is to devote it to the service of God in return. So he put it up to the Salvation Army — told them how God had wrought a miracle for him, tried to make them see how this flying goat was proof of the power of prayer, asked them to come and see it for themselves. Up to that time he'd kept it secret. Now he wanted all the world to know about it. Well, they were very sniffy, the Salvation Armyists. It looked like sacrilege. The power of prayer and miracle was kept for serious things — healing, faith, help in time of trouble, sin and sorrow and so on. A flying goat looked a bit like taking

184

a rise out of the Almighty. Well, they argued and disagreed and then argued again, but at last Jethro persuaded them. The Salvation Armyists gathered in a field behind Jethro's house and waited for the goat to fly. It didn't do anything. It didn't even lift its feet off the ground. Well, just what we thought, they said, just what we expected. The man has not only made fools of us but has taken the name of God in vain. We'll see about this, and they did, to the extent that Jethro never set foot in the Salvation Army hall again and never played the euphonium for them any more.

"But still," I said, "the goat could fly?"

Yes, he said, the goat could fly. It flew better and better as it grew older and older. Jethro never trained it. Just fed it and it flew. The only thing Jethro used to do was whistle it home, and then when it came home it used to circle round and round like a homing pigeon. Well, soon after the Salvation Armyists turned him down Jethro had another idea. He decided to take the goat on tour. That's how he got in with the circus. At first,

Jethro told me, they didn't believe him. Then when they saw that goat flying over a circus tent the circus folk went crazy. It was just the craziest thing ever seen in a circus. Better than man-eating lions, performing seals, dancing ponies and all that. Everybody had seen things like that, but nobody had ever seen a flying goat. It was a sensation. It went everywhere. Everywhere you went you saw the circus-bills about Jethro Watkins's flying goat.

"It's funny I never heard of it," I said.

Funny, he said, I should think it is funny. Everybody's heard of Jethro Watkins's flying goat. Everybody.

"Except me," I said. "Well, what happened then?"

Well, Jethro thought he could do better for himself than the circus. So he struck out on his own. And that began the real sensational stuff. You know, flying off the top of the Tower at Blackpool and all that. You mean to say you never heard of that?

"No," I said, "I can't say I ever heard of it."

It was in all the newspapers, he said.

Pictures of it. Millions of people there. Don't you know what happened? A newspaper offered Jethro five thousand pounds if the goat would fly off the top of the Tower. Well, it flew off the top of the Tower and flew round over the sea for a few minutes and then settled on the pier. But that was nothing. You must have heard all about the time when it flew away from Belle Vue Manchester and was missing over the Pennines for a night and a day and then came flying home to Jethro's old home here as cool as you like? Why, he said, that was the biggest sensation of the lot.

"I bet it was," I said. "Now tell me it flew the Channel."

Well, it did, he said, but that isn't what I was going to tell you about. I was going to tell you about the time it had kids.

"Don't tell me they could fly," I said.

One could, he said, but not the other. That was funny, wasn't it? One kid was black, and one was white, and it was the white one that could fly. Jethro said it was marvellous. Better than the mother. The second day after it was born Jethro took it out and it flew twice round the church steeple. Well, if a goat could do that on the second day of its life, what was it going to do when it was a year old?

"You tell me," I said. "I don't know."

Well, he said, that was the sad thing. Jethro died. He was always a fat chap and I think he must have got fatty heart or something. Anyway the day he got the young goat to loop the loop the excitement must have been too much for him. He dropped down dead.

"The excitement," I said, "would have been too much for anybody. What happened to the goats after Jethro died?"

Well, he said, that's another funny thing. Nobody seems to know.

"They just flew away," I said. "Is that it?"

Well, nobody knows, he said. There were a lot of goats sold at auction after Jethro was dead, but none of them could fly.

"How many times did you see the flying goat?" I said. "I mean you, yourself."

Well, he said.

"Didn't you ever see it at all?"

Well, he said, to tell the truth I didn't. I heard all about it, but I never got the chance to see it.

"Didn't you ever know anybody who saw it?" I said.

No, he said, I can't say I did. Not exactly.

"Well," I said, "didn't you ever know anybody who knew anybody who'd seen it?"

No, he said, if it comes to that, I didn't. Not exactly.

"Then," I said, "tell me who told you all about it?"

Jethro, he said.

I didn't say anything this time.

Don't you believe it? he said.

"Oh! yes," I said, "I believe it."

After all, he said, it takes no more believing than the feeding of five thousand people with two loaves and five small fishes, does it?

"Oh, no!" I said.

After all, he said, you can make yourself believe in anything if you want to, can't you?

"Oh! yes!" I said.

Well, he said, it's been very nice. I think I'll be getting along.

"No, you don't," I said. "Wait a minute. Just sit down. It's my turn to tell you something. I'd like to tell you about my uncle Walter's musical pig. Now when I was a boy my uncle Walter had a pig that played the trombone. I don't mean it was a pig that played the trombone with the trombone. I mean it was a pig that played the trombone without a trombone. Now this pig had a litter — "

The Late Public Figure

THE offices of the *Argus and Express* Printing Works, which printed and had printed for forty-five years *The Nulborough Weekly Argus and Express*, were in a state of excitement. The proprietor, founder and at one time editor of the paper, Mr. Charles Macauley Montague, a public figure in the town, had died suddenly in the night.

In the front office, which had been partitioned off from the printing rooms by a match-boarding partition, varnished yellow, the editor, Stacey, was beating the fist of first one hand, then another, then both, on the edge of the varnished roll-top desk. It was a hot day in August and the heat of weeks had burnt the walls against the fly-specked windows to soft blisters. Resin had long since oozed, for the same reason, out of the pine knots, to be boiled to reddish blisters which past summers had dried and cracked.

The panels of thick ridged glass in the factory-type windows somehow let in the heat and then imprisoned it. The catches of the windows would not open and dust lay thick on the obsolete files and unpinned lays of galleys, on the desks and windowsills, and on the ancient handle-type wall telephone. Across the ceiling a steel shafting ran and revolved, let in and out of the room by two holes cut in the match-board partition like holes in a fowl-house. Mysteriously propelled, bright as a silver pencil, this piece of machinery seemed the only up-to-date thing, and certainly the only clean thing, in the office, which smelled like a long shut book suddenly opened in a chapel-pew. The place had the air of some ill-managed dead letter office long behind the times, ill-conditioned, unprosperous and hopelessly lost. Yet for forty-five years, back to the week when the first file had been pinned up in 1892, *The Argus and Express* had been run at a profit. Stacey, the editor, knew all about this, had seen the books, and knew that Mr. Charles Macauley Montague would leave about, perhaps, fifty thousand pounds. What he did not know, beyond this, was anything very much about Mr. Montague himself. He realized that he did not know enough to write the obituary notice the occasion demanded.

"I tell you I've got to know something about him! Don't you see?" He beat his fists on the edge of the table as he talked to Hanson, the works manager. "I want a special. An obituary number. I want to put his career in, his history — what he's done, what he's been! And all you can do is to stand there and say you don't know anything. To-day's Thursday and the dead line's to-morrow morning."

"You've been here as long as I have, Mr. Stacey. Six years."

"Yes, I know. But you've lived here. In the town. All your life."

"Yes, but — "

"All right, all right." Stacey took up a paper from the desk. He was a young man with very black hair and a pale yellow face, with the sun-tired oily eyes of someone who had spent too long, at one time, in the tropics. He had spent two years editing a paper in Madras, from

193

where he had gone, for another three years, to Calcutta. Yet the heat of the *Argus* office seemed to him impossibly terrific, unbearable. The back-glaze from the shining yellow varnish hurt his eyes, kindling the fatigue behind them.

"All right," he said. "If you don't know anything perhaps you can check these facts. Say 'No' if I'm wrong." He began to read from the paper: "Aged 71, founded *Argus* in 1892, chairman Liberal Association 1906 – 14 elected Urban District Council 1919, chairman 1925, continued in council till death, vice-chairman League of Nations Union Local Branch 1925 – 30, Church Trustee Baptist Church 1920 – 32, sidesman similar period, president Local Temperance Reform Committee 1895 – 1914, active interest Moral Welfare 1920 onwards, active interest Young Men's Christian Association similar period, Carnegie Library Committee 1923 – 30, speaker and later chairman Pleasant Saturday Evenings commencing 1893, surrendered editorship of paper 1930."

He ceased reading. The works manager did not speak. "Well, all correct?"

The works manager said yes, he thought it was all correct.

"But that's just his activities," Stacey said. "I want the *man*. The personality. You know anything about that? I mean about how he was educated, how he started? He wasn't married, was he? You know why he came here? What made him choose this dead-alive hole to start a paper in?"

"No, Mr. Stacey, I don't."

"Is there anybody in the works who would know?"

The works manager thought a moment. "Rankin might. He started here as a boy. He — "

"All right! Send Rankin up."

While the works manager had gone Stacey took off his coat and with his fists tried hard to bang open a window, to let in some air. The windows seemed as if screwed down and would not budge. He sat down at the table in an ill-temper and turned over papers not seeing what he read.

Then the door opened and Rankin, a small man of sixty, foreman of the downstairs room, came in. He was a man who did not say much and was even then a long time saying it. His words were like a jumble of pins, which he had to sort out, and then stick in, slowly, but sharply, so that there should be no mistaking their point.

"You knew Mr. Montague a long time?" Stacey said.

"Longer," Rankin said, and slowly he stuck in the pins of his words, his eyes slightly ironic behind his black-rimmed glasses, "than you'd think."

"What was his personal history? You know anything about his activities in this town besides his Liberal Association and church affairs — things like that?"

Rankin, thought, then spoke. "He was our landlord."

"What's that got to do with it?"

"You know," Rankin said, "where I live? In Lime Street?"

Stacey had a vision of small bay-windows, fern-decorated, in a little boulevard of limes.

"Not trees," Rankin said. "Just lime — ordinary lime. There was a pit there once, and then it petered out, and a man named Hobbs put up two rows of houses.

Mr. Montague owned that property."

"That's interesting, but — "

"You ought to see our house. I go to dinner," Rankin said, "at half-past twelve. Come in and have a look at us about one."

Stacey said, without really meaning it, that he would go in. The slow careful speech of Rankin bored him a little. He wanted to open the door on the pretext of getting some air and so let the man out, but suddenly Rankin was talking again, rather faster.

"You wouldn't remember," he said, "the soldiers we had billeted on us during the war, would you? The first battalion Royal Welch. They came in 1915. December, just before Christmas. They marched here — marched thirty-five miles, and it rained and sleeted all the way, nine hours."

"Yes," Stacey said, "but what has it got to do with Mr. Montague?"

"I'm trying to tell you," Rankin said, in his slow pin-pricking voice. "You ever seen soldiers after a nine-hour march in the rain? Them chaps couldn't have been wetter if they walked all day in rivers.

We had three billeted on us — kids, about eighteen. And Mr. Montague and his sister had three. It upset my missus, seeing them boys. She rushed out and got mutton bones and had hot stew ready by the time they'd had a bath in the kitchen. Of course you wasn't supposed to do things like that for 'em. They'd got regulation rations, and all that. But you couldn't sit still and see kids starved through and not do a thing."

"You seem to have forgotten," Stacey said, with patience, "that you're talking about Mr. Montague."

"No, no," Rankin said. "No. Everybody in Nulborough did the same for them boys — got 'em stew and tea and cocoa and all the like o' that — everybody. All except Mr. Montague."

Stacey did not speak. He sat quite still. He felt a small aperture in his mind open and let in a small slit of light.

"All except Mr. Montague," Rankin said, "and Miss Montague. No stew for them kids, no cocoa, not a drop o' tea. No bath. You couldn't wonder what happened — one of 'em got pneumonia and died, and in a week the other two asked to be moved."

Stacey, watching the small aperture of light in his mind grow larger, could not speak. Then Rankin said a surprising, irrelevant thing.

"He never had more than half an egg for his breakfast. Mr. Montague half an egg, Miss Montague half an egg."

Rankin stood silent, looking at Stacey. It was as though he had finished sticking in the pins of his words, as though he had at last made a pattern of them, like the pattern on a pin-table. He seemed to stand there and say: "Now it's your turn. You shoot. See if you can get the ball in the right hole," his small ironical print-black eyes speaking for him.

Stacey did not speak, and Rankin, after asking if there was anything more that he needed, turned to go. Stacey stopped him at the door.

"You know anybody else," he said, "who might tell me anything?"

Rankin said: "Miss Montague might." He paused. "I say she might. But Brierley's the man you ought to see. Started here as compositor in 1892 and worked himself up to manager. Left just before you came. I say left."

"Where's he live?"

"Eighteen Denmark Street. You'll pass it on the way up to Miss Montague."

As Rankin left the office, Stacey remembered something and called after him: "I'll drop in and see you about one." Alone, he contemplated the small aperture of light in his mind. He tried to bring pressure on it, as he had done on the window, in order to make it open wider. In this uncertain state of mind, he got his keys out of his desk and unlocked the door which led into Mr. Montague's office and went in. He looked cursorily over Mr. Montague's desk and went to open and shut one or two of the pigeon-drawers, not at first reading anything. Then journalistic curiosity got the better of him, and he sat down on the old-fashioned swivel-chair and began to read, here and there, some of Mr. Montague's papers. He found a copy of Mr. Montague's birth certificate; it showed his registration as a child in a small town in the county of Essex, his father a solicitor's clerk, his mother described as a machinist. The date was 1865. In the same drawer he found envelopes containing copies of Mr. Montague's life policies. Below them were letters from Mr. Montague's London brokers, and from them it seemed that Mr. Montague had held substantial holdings in steel generally, and in arms particularly. One letter acknowledged the transference, in Mr. Montague's name, of some £8000 from investment in Public Utilities to investment in the share organizations manufacturing arms. Turning over more papers, Stacey came across a series of hotel bills. These were all for hotels in various parts of London, but appeared otherwise to have nothing to do with each other. Then Stacey noticed that they were bills, always, for double rooms taken and vacated on the same days of the week, Friday and Saturday. In another drawer he found two bills, both from the same hotel, dated as recently as July of the current year. The hotel was near Paddington Station and he put one of the bills in his pocket.

In his own office the telephone rang.

Answering it, he heard the crackling echo of Miss Montague's voice. He had already spoken to her once that morning, to convey the regrets of convention. Now he heard her asking if he would go up and see her. He said he would be there in half an hour.

Hot air pressed down on him in a series of dusty waves as he spoke into the antiquated wall mouthpiece. Hanging up the receiver, he made one more effort to open the window, banging it with his fist, so that the office would be fresh when he came back. The window would not budge.

He went downstairs, gave instructions that he would be out till 1.30, and then backed his car out of the cinder-yard running up by the works entrance. He calculated that he could give the man named Brierley twenty minutes and still arrive punctually for Miss Montague.

Denmark Street ran along the old part of the town, by the now culverted river, just before a steep rise in the land. Beyond it short streets rose steeply to the district popularized by the pre-war manufacturers, who had built large red-brick laurel-encompassed houses in what had then been cheap land. Brierley's house was number eighteen in a row of thirty-six. They were old stone houses rendered over with thin pumice-coloured cement, against the dampness of the river flowing partly underneath them.

Brierley's door was opened by a young man of twenty-six or more, whose face to Stacey seemed partially familiar. He had a screw-driver and a coil of insulated wire in his hands, and inside the room Stacey could see the man he took to be Brierley, sitting at a table strewn with the parts of a dismantled wireless set.

"Mr. Brierley?" Stacey said. "I dropped in to tell you that Mr. Montague was dead. Perhaps you heard."

Brierley got up from the table. He was dressed in engineer's blue overalls, a big man, with a greasy face and bright grey eyes that were like polished machine bearings. "Come in a minute," he said, and Stacey stepped straight from the street into the room, telling Brierley, as he automatically wiped his shoes on the door-mat, who he was.

"I've got to get an obituary notice, and a pretty big one, for to-morrow," he said. "You were with Mr. Montague a long time and I thought perhaps you could tell me something."

"Yes," Brierley said, "I could tell you something." He looked at Stacey with eyes that were as bright but as dead as steel. Then suddenly they were alive, angrily set in motion. "For a start," he said, "I'll tell you what to write at the top o' that notice. Write — 'A Bloody Good Job'. Write that."

Stacey became aware again of the aperture of light in his mind. He looked at Brierley's eyes. He remembered another man he had interviewed, in Madras, after a railway accident in which the young girl he was about to marry had lain for two hours with crushed legs. He saw the same energy of pained fury generated in Brierley's eyes with the same inability to escape, to spring out of the latent flesh and direct itself. It occurred to him suddenly that the balls of Brierley's eyes could slot into the pattern made by Rankin's pins: the two were connected, component, springing from the same hatred.

"Sit down," Brierley said. He looked at the young man. "You'd better go and get that detector valve," he said. "We shan't get much forrader without it."

The young man went out, and Stacey, the impression of familiarity still with him, sat looking after him, semi-consciously. Then Brierley sat down and they looked at each other across the litter of tools, screws, wireless parts. Brierley's eyes were still.

"Anything else you'd like me to put?" Stacey said.

"Yes." Brierley said, slowly. "Find out the bloody truth and put that in."

"I'd like to. But — "

"Put that kid in," Brierley said. "Yes, him. My daughter's kid. — Montague's kid. That's *one* bit of truth you can put in."

Stacey sat quiet, his mind clear. "And another bit?"

"Add up," Brierley said, "the interest on a hundred and twenty-five quid for thirty-six years."

"What's that got to do with it?"

Brierley said: "Montague came here and started in a small way in 1892. In 1899 he was a bit rocky and he asked if I'd lend him some money. I'd just had a hundred and fifty left me by an old uncle up in Sheffield — so I lent him a hundred and twenty-five. Well, I was green and never asked for an agreement and he never suggested it. When I asked for repayment he said, 'I'll make you foreman and give you a ten shilling rise and pay it back that way.' Like a fool I took it. Then he got on a bit and started the paper and I asked him if he'd give my daughter a job. She was eighteen then. Well, he gave her a job in the office — meant late hours, but she liked it. Then you see what happened."

They looked at each other, the bright machine eyes of Brierley, livid with the furious but directionless power of the revived hatred. "But you did something about that?" Stacey said. "Made Montague pay?"

"No," Brierley said. "He denied it. Then he half admitted it, but said that if we done anything I should lose my job. Well, there was only one printing works in this town then."

There was nothing, Stacey felt, that he could say; but in his mind he began to see the small steel balls of one circumstance and another falling into the holes made by the imaginary pattern of Rankin's words. He picked up his hat and got up to go. Brierley got up also.

"You know I can't put it in," Stacey said.

"Yes, I know! And he knew. When you get back to the office you look up the files. Read the bloody editorials. I set every one of 'em up for nearly forty years. Read the council reports, Moral Welfare, every damn thing, also who gets the biscuit every time? Montague, always Montague. He knew there were things you couldn't print."

Stacey could not say anything. He shook hands with Brierley. The large heavy-veined hands of the older man were trembling. Then Brierley opened his mouth as though to say something else, but refrained, and Stacey knew that there was still something else, something important and perhaps painful, which had not been said.

He went out into the street, into the hot sunshine. He drove the car up the hill, coming to the Montague house in about five minutes. Set back behind a hedge of laurel and a small plantation of lime and pink may and covered almost entirely with virginia creeper, the house revealed no character. He walked up the gravel drive, pulled the brass doorbell, and was shown finally into the drawing-room, where Miss Montague was waiting for him. The blinds of the room were drawn and the whole effect — the yellowish light, the rarefied silence, the semi-stale smell of upholstery, all reminded him of the East. He had interviewed many second-rate opera singers, in many such shaded and faded rooms, in Calcutta.

Miss Montague, a straight hipped, thin woman already all in black, with a square gold locket at her neck, looked ill. She struck him as being a woman who had for years concealed the fact that she thought for herself. Her mind was like a prayer book with a safety clasp: tight-shut, secure, hiding something, hiding perhaps the texts of old resolves and ambitions and even desires. She looked hungry, not merely emotionally and mentally, but physically. She looked as if she had lived, for the past twenty years, on sandwiches of india-paper. He remembered Rankin, the half egg for breakfast, the wartime story of meanness. It astonished him to see no meanness in Miss Montague's face, but only, uppermost, a look of hungry martyrdom.

He felt hungry himself, having breakfasted at his lodgings at eight. The hot sunshine had tired him, and he would have been glad of a cup of coffee.

He sat down on the sofa, carefully, between the geometrically placed cushions of dark plum velvet, and Miss Montague sat in a chair opposite. They had already exchanged the formal regrets over the telephone. Now she simply said:

"It is very good of you to come. This afternoon I expect the relations. I have been on my feet since half-past four."

He heard in the voice the same skin-and-bone expression as he saw in her face. For want of something to say, he threw out a large hint about some refreshment.

Much to his surprise she took it. She said: "Perhaps that's what's the matter with me. I haven't eaten since last night. I came over faint a few minutes ago. Could you eat something, Mr. Stacey?"

"I feel so hungry," he said, "I could eat a plate of fried eggs."

She looked startled. Fear and temptation, with some kind of hesitant courage, filled and emptied her eyes.

"You could?" she said.

"I could!"

She seemed to think, to weigh the consequences of a decision. Then: "I believe I could," she said, "myself."

She got up and pulled the porcelain bell-handle by the fireplace, and when the girl answered, said:

"Oh, Emily. I think I could eat some breakfast now. Mr. Stacey is going to have some with me. We are going to have bacon and eggs. Have we some rashers?"

"Only two, Miss. It's Thursday."

"Don't worry about me. I never eat more than one rasher," Stacey said.

"I could do some fried bread, Miss," the girl said.

"Fried bread," Miss Montague said. "You like fried bread, Mr. Stacey?"

"I love it."

"Could you eat one egg or two?"

"Well, thank you," Stacey said, "I

think I could eat two eggs."

"And some tea, Emily, please," Miss Montague said. "On the small table in here."

As they sat waiting for the meal to come, Stacey explained his intentions: how he would devote the two whole middle pages of the paper, suitably black edged, to Mr. Montague, outlining his career, his achievements in spheres of social activity. He explained how he had already sent out his reporters to get, from important local people, tributes to Mr. Montague's life and work and how he would print these tributes in three or perhaps four columns. He explained how he himself would write the obituary notice, the tribute that would express the loss of a paper, the employees and the community.

"But," he said, "I don't want to do anything you don't approve. Also there must be many things about Mr. Montague which you could tell me. Things which would help me to write the article."

She sat looking at the wall with tired, hungry eyes, careful not to look at him.

He waited for her to say something, but she sat completely silent. He recalled Rankin, Brierley, who had both spoken so readily. He saw how hard it was, one way or another, for her to say anything at all.

He began to question her, gently, in an impersonal fashion that would not hurt her. He thought he was correct in saying that Mr. Montague was seventy-one?

"Yes," she said.

"He had come to the town in 1892? I just want to verify these facts."

"Yes, in 1892."

"He had not been married at all?"

"No."

"Had Mr. Montague any other interests outside the town and the paper? Had he any interests in London?"

"No," she said. Then she altered her mind. "Well, if you call it an interest, he used to go up to London every Friday to discuss affairs with an old friend. A Mr. Clarkson."

"Do you yourself know Mr. Clarkson?"

"No," Miss Montague said, "I never met him."

Very shortly afterwards the breakfast

came. The girl said she had put the fried bread on a separate plate. Miss Montague thanked her and then lifted the covers and began to help Stacey to eggs and bread and bacon. She was looking now at the eggs, and he saw in her eyes again the same ebb and flow of guilt and temptation, pursued by courage, that he had seen before. Something made him say:

"You know, I don't think I can eat two eggs, after all, my mother always used to say my eyes were bigger than my" — he wanted to say 'belly', but couldn't — "stomach. You eat the other."

She hesitated and he saw her lips trembling: he knew she was crying with anxiety, inwardly, frightened. He coaxed her: "You haven't eaten since last night," and then, at first slowly, then quickly, in a fashion meant to be quite debonair, she took the egg.

She began to eat. At first she ate daintily, with circumspect rabbit-movements of her thin lips, then more quickly, then quite rapidly, the golden egg-icicles hanging on her fork and lips and dropping down before she could lick them off. He saw the bacon fat shining, forgotten, on her chin, the shine very like the look in her eyes, a look of gleaming, unadulterated pleasure. And he knew that he was watching her, for the first time in her life, eat two eggs off the same plate, at the same time.

They each drank three or four cups of tea. Miss Montague at last sat back with an expression of almost bloated repletion. Two eggs, a rasher and three slices of fried bread, washed down by tea, had puffed, very slightly, the starved bagginess under her eyes. She was full up, blown out, and the effect on her was like that of a small dissipation. She got out her handkerchief and held it to her mouth, and Stacey saw her stifle a series of small belches behind it.

The look of repletion in her flushed eyes reminded him of something, but he could not think what. But suddenly he thought of something else: he realized that she had told him nothing of Mr. Montague himself. So he put another question: "What had been Mr. Montague's relation to the arts? Music, for instance, books, painting?"

"Music he didn't care for," she said. "Nor painting, I think. He read a lot, at night, in bed. Most of his books are in his study upstairs."

"You care for music?" Stacey said.

"Oh! yes, very much. Very much. I — "

She stopped. The thought, the sentence and the resolution to tell him something all collapsed. Her mind shut itself up, tight, behind its prayer-book clasp, so that nothing should fall out.

"I'm afraid I can't be much help to you," she said.

"No?"

"He never took me very much into his confidence."

He was about to ask another question when he remembered something. The remembrance was evoked by the puffed full-stomach look in her eyes. He had it clear, now, what it was he had been trying to remember. It was a recollection of Mr. Montague himself, at the anniversary dinner of the Local Fire Brigade. He saw Mr. Montague eating at the long white table like one of a litter of forty shirt-fronted pigs, sucking the food into his mouth nervously, as though in fear he would be pushed from the trough. The look in and under his eyes, puffed and slightly flushed, was exactly the look on Miss Montague's face: a look of hunger, in his own case intensified by greed, satisfied at last. He saw the pork gravy rushing down the bony chin, the grease like oil on the moustache ends, the eyes slightly protuberant, as though in an effort to magnify the food on the plate.

He came back to the drawing-room. He knew that he had already asked her enough. He put a last question:

"May I see Mr. Montague's books?"

"They're mostly under lock and key," she said. "He prized some of them greatly. But you can go up, of course."

She led him up the once white but now bone-coloured stairs. Up above, it was silent, and he could feel the presence, like a long-held breath, of the dead man. Except for this, the whole house seemed empty, a house of bone, hollow, from which flesh and marrow had been starved out. In this bare skeleton he pictured Mr. and Miss Montague living, for forty years, on half an egg a day.

She showed him into the study. "You just look round the books," she said, "while I go and speak to the maid. I have so much to do."

When she had gone he looked round the study, saw the rows of dull books, theological, political, memoirs of London journalists, on the leather-fringed bookshelves. The room held two bureaux, with wooden cupboards on top. In one of the cupboards Stacey saw a key and curiosity made him turn it and open the cupboard and look inside. Again, many books.

Stacey did not touch them. He stood looking at their titles. Not quite astonished, he read: *The Symbols of Eroticism, Love and Beauty, The Art of Love, Full Womanhood, Love and Woman, Seventy Art Studies (From Life), Erotica Ancient and Modern*. There were others, perhaps a hundred or a hundred and twenty volumes. Stacey did not touch them. He locked the cupboard, hesitated about the key, then left it in the lock and went downstairs.

"He was a great reader," Miss Montague

said, when she met him at the foot of the stairs.

"Have you a photograph of him?" Stacey said.

"There is a very good one of him, taken at the Church Conference," she said.

"Yes, I think we've got a block of that."

"I daresay there were others," she said.

"As a young man?"

"Perhaps I could look something out," she said, "and send it down to the office?"

He thanked her, said he would see that she saw a proof of his article by eight o'clock on the following morning — the paper would not be on the streets until afternoon — and said good-bye. She looked at him sadly, with the habitual hungriness ingrained into her bones and flesh by years of under-nourishment, of acquiescent and perhaps, he thought, terrorized starvation. Then just as he was going, she smiled. It was the furtive semi-guilty smile of someone who has done something a trifle reckless, in a momentary spasm of abandonment. The yellow splash of egg-yolk had dried vivid on her chin.

Driving down the hill, back to the town, he only just remembered his promise to Rankin. He turned off from the hill and, in about three minutes, came to Lime Street. 'Mr. Montague owns that property', he remembered.

He looked at the property. Two rows of dog-kennels ran parallel down a steep slope. A notice prohibiting heavy traffic stood at one end. Kids were playing, snot-nosed, on the street and on the two-feet pavement; shoe hands sat on the door-steps, in the shade, waiting for the afternoon buzzers.

Stacey found No. 12, Rankin's house, and went up the entry and round to the back door. Rankin was sitting in his shirt sleeves at the dinner-table, and called, 'Come in'.

Stacey went in. "The missus has just gone into next door," Rankin said. "That just leaves room for you."

Stacey looked round the room.

"You ever keep dogs in a kennel?" Rankin said, in his dry, pin-pricking way.

Stacey knew there was no need to answer, no need to comment on the miserable smallness of the room, with the old-fashioned upright gas-mantle on the wall, the broken ceiling, the varnished and re-varnished wall-paper rubbed off, here and there, by years of passing elbows.

"If you smell anything," Rankin said, "It's just a stink."

"What's the rent?" Stacey said.

"Eleven and six. Began at four and six. Montague itched it up and up till it was thirteen and six, one time. But they stopped that."

"How many more rooms?"

"Oh! tremendous number," Rankin said. "Come on, I'll show you."

Rankin showed him the little extra front room. Even on that hot day, Stacey was shocked by its coldness. Rankin pulled back the linoleum, showing it blue-green, mould-furred, on the under side. He pulled up a floor board. On the joist, underneath, he showed Stacey the marks of rats' teeth, and, on the bare earth lower down, the marks of rats' feet and many rat-droppings. "I'd take you upstairs," Rankin said, "but the missus would die. Come outside."

Stacey followed Rankin into the yard. Rankin showed him the little community water-closet, the old-fashioned iron yard water tap. "Mr. Montague owned the property," he said.

Then: "Did Brierley tell you anything?"

"Yes."

"Everything?"

"No."

"He wouldn't tell you about the girl dying?"

"That was it."

Stacey felt that there was nothing more to say. Rankin's slow words had made another pattern of pins in his mind, and he could see the pins, now, very bright in the wider aperture of light.

He drove Rankin back to the office. They came up out of Lime Street like men coming up from a culvert for air. The heat of the day, in the higher streets, was sweet.

"Ever hear Mr. Montague talk of anyone named Clarkson?" Stacey said.

"No," Rankin said, "I can't say I did."

Obsessed by the name, for some reason, Stacey went upstairs to his office. The imprisoned heat struck at him in a muffled cloud as he went in. He stood on a chair and again, as in the morning, tried to beat open the window with his fists, but without success.

Then he went into Mr. Montague's office, sat down at his desk, and tried to find some evidence of the name Clarkson. As he searched, he kept coming across the Paddington hotel bills, always for the same night, Friday, always for the double room.

He went back into his own office. The reporters had been in with notes, urgent queries, which they had left on his desk. He scanned them, scribbled replies on them and then telephoned down to the composing room that he would be out again until 7 or 8 o'clock that evening, and that he would work all night.

Then he looked up the trains to London. There was one at 1.53 which would bring him into Euston at 3.11. He caught this train.

The woman who came to the door of the Paddington hotel, that afternoon, asked him at once:

"Room? Double or single?"

Like Miss Montague, the woman was also in black, and her mind, like hers, seemed clasped tight shut, so that nothing should escape from it. But the closing up of her mind was conscious.

"I would like to know if you ever knew a Mr. Montague?" he said.

"Mr. Montague, Mr. Montague," she said. "No, no." She thought again. "No."

"Is this one of your hotel-bills?" he said.

She looked at the bill. "Oh! yes, oh yes. That's one of our bills."

While she was looking at the bill, he took out the photograph of Mr. Montague taken at the Annual Church Conference, and gave it her. "Would you know that gentleman?"

"That?" she said. "I should say so! That's one of our regular clients. Mr. Clarkson."

"That's right," Stacey said. "This Mr. Clarkson was a friend of Mr. Montague. That's what I was trying to get at."

"Nothing wrong, I hope?" she said.

He told her then that Mr. Montague,

Mr. Clarkson, was dead.

"Oh! poor Mrs. Clarkson!"

Stacey did not say anything.

"Sudden?"

He told her how sudden it was. "They often came here?" he said.

"Oh! yes. But don't stand out here in the hot sun," she said, and he followed her into the hotel, with its hat-stand in the hall, the stale odours of greasy meals, the hush of afternoon. She looked into the lounge. It was empty, and she invited him in.

"Oh! poor Mrs. Clarkson."

Casually, Stacey asked about Mrs. Clarkson. What was she like?

"Smart," the woman said, "Long hands. Much younger than Mr. Clarkson. Very smart."

"Had they been married long?"

"I think about seven or eight years. Of course Mr. Clarkson used to come here before that. Oh yes. He came here quite often with the first Mrs. Clarkson."

Stacey asked what the first Mrs. Clarkson was like.

"Oh! a much different woman. Plumper. A bit coarse. Common. A type. You could see what she wanted."

"She died?" Stacey said.

"Oh! no, no. I don't think so. A divorce, I think. Oh! yes it was a divorce. I know we thought it was a very good thing for Mr. Clarkson at the time."

"Thank you." He picked up his hat.

"Won't you have a cup of tea?" she said. "I didn't ask you."

He thanked her, said no, and went out into the street. As she let him out of the shabby hotel lobby he knew her eyes were filling with tears and he tried not to notice it. "We shall miss him," she said. "He had such a way with him."

There was nothing else he could do. He caught the earliest train back from Euston at 6.30, having a wash and some tea on the train so that he could drive straight to the office.

It was just after half-past seven when he arrived at the office and now, as in the morning and afternoon, the pent up heat of the day struck at him as soon as he opened the door.

He sat down at his deck, tired, and looked at the day's accumulation of papers: the notes brought in by reporters, others sent up by the composing room, and among them the photograph of Mr. Montague, as a young man, sent along by Miss Montague.

He sat looking at the photograph. "This would have been taken," Miss Montague's note said, "about 1893." Mr. Montague was wearing a straw-hat, a white crocheted tie and cream flannel trousers held up by a wide fancy waist-band. The face was full lipped, the eyes very black, like ripe berries, and the nostrils wide and sensuous. Stacey looked at it.

Suddenly he could not bear the heat any longer. He got up and banged at the window with his fists again. It would not open. Then his persistent knocking split off a wafer of sun-burned paint, and he saw underneath it the head of a screw. He saw then that the window had been screwed up for years.

He went down to the engine-room and borrowed a screw-driver from the engineer and then, scraping off more paint, at last had the screws clear, so that he could turn them. There were four screws and in five minutes he had taken them out. The window opened easily then, and he left it open and the clear evening air began to come in, slowly, very sweet, out of the August dusk, clarifying the room and giving it new life.

He sat down at his desk. The tributes to Mr. Montague as a public figure, from many prominent public figures, had come in and were laid under a paper weight. He took them up and read them through.

Then, refilling his pen and taking up a pile of the obsolete pink election-ballot sheets always used in that office, by Mr. Montague's orders, for the sake of economy, he began to write his notice.

He took his tone from the tributes to a public figure. Filling his lungs with the fresh August night air, he wrote:

'It is with the profoundest regret that we learn, to-day, of the sudden and untimely death of Mr. Charles Macauley Montague, founder, proprietor, and editor for forty-five years of this paper, and for almost all of that time a public figure.'

The Blind

ONCE a week, every market day, the man Osborn and his wife drove down to the town in the old Ford tourer piled up with chicken crates, to take their girl to the travelling optician. They called him the eye-doctor. "Now then, look slippy," the man would say. "We don' wan' keep th'eye doctor waiting," or the woman: "You think th'eye doctor's got all day to wait? Git y' things on quick. Look about you." But they were never late. Punctually at half-past nine the car came down into the town, mud-spattered or chalk white from its journey across the field-track from the poultry farm, the man with rusty moustaches hanging down like loose tobacco from the pouch of his mouth; the woman like a hen herself with beak-nose and cherry-hung hat bobbing like a comb; and the girl sitting between them on the cart-cushion, staring with still stone-coloured eyes into the distance, as though she could see beyond the ends of the earth.

"Summat do wi' cat's eyes." The man had become slightly addicted to boasting about it. He had a habit of blowing into his moustaches, with a sound of astonishment. "Knock-out, ain't it? Think as the gal's got eyes like that? He reckons it gonna take about eight or nine months to cure it. Seven and six a time — that's money."

The eye-doctor rented the front room of a house behind the market. He hung his card in the window, above the fern pots. 'J. I. Varipatana. Optician. Attendance Tuesdays 10 a.m. – 1 p.m. 2 p.m. – 4 p.m.' And punctually at ten o'clock he would come to open the door to them, with the shell-white smile dazzling on his dusky sand-coloured face, his dark hand extended, and his way of greeting them with impersonal courtesy.

"Mrs. Osborn. Mr. Osborn. Miss Osborn. Please enter."

In the front room a number of cards with test numbers hung on the wall facing the light. The eye-doctor stood with his hands clasped behind his back, the white almost feminine smile constantly on his dark face. "And how is business with Mister Osborn? Nice weather. And Mrs. Osborn? You look very well. And the little lady?"

The girl sat as though far away, dumb.

"Well, speak up. Th'eye doctor's speaking to you. Lost your tongue?"

"The eyes are a little better?"

"Yes," the girl would say.

"Good. Very good. Very good." The voice slow, correct, rather beautiful. "You persevered with the lotion?"

"Yes."

"Come near the window."

He would hold back one curtain a little, so that the light fell on the stone-coloured, almost dead eyes. "Yes. Look up to me. Now shut the eyes. Now open. Look out of the window. Look just like that for one minute. Yes." The voice soft, in rumination, sauvely gentle. "Now shut them again. Open now. Look sideways."

And then, as she looked sideways, he would put his hands on her face, the fingers supporting her head, the thumbs touching the eyelids. Like that he would look down at her, still smiling, until the force of his own eyes drew her own back again. With his thumbs he peeled back the lids and then released them. The man and woman watched in silence, waiting for the verdict.

"The cataract is no worse." The smile remained on the lips, even as they spoke and shut. "Indeed perhaps a little better."

By silence they demonstrated their complete faith in him. They saw him as someone who could perform a miracle. Still more, the girl took on importance because it was on her that the miracle was being performed. And they, in turn, took importance from her.

One week the women grew impatient, impelled by fear. "Ain't she never goin' to git no better?"

"My dear Mrs. Osborn." The voice itself had something miraculous in it, some gentle hypnotic healing quality. "I am not a magician. The eyes are very precious, very delicate. You see, think of it like this. If you cut your finger I can put something on it that will heal, that will destroy the germs. Some iodine, something to burn out the infection. But no — not on the eyes. No drastic measures can cure the eyes. Only time and faith can cure the eyes. You must be patient, and have faith."

Continually, week by week, the girl herself had the impression that she could see less. At a distance of forty feet hung a curtain of mist that her eyes could not penetrate, and gradually, she felt, this mist began to close in on her. She began to see the hens at home only as vague lumps of colour, and on dull days, when the light was poor, the black hens were lost on her altogether. The hens, which she fed morning and evening, were the test for her, and gradually, with the range of vision lessening, she had to begin to rely less on sight than hearing. By hearing, by listening to the sound of hen noises, her mind conjured the vision that eyes could not see. She began to hear things with wonderful clarity.

In the eye-doctor's small front-room there were no hens, no test for her. And she was always frightened. Partly through fear, partly through some notion that if she said a thing often enough it would eventually become a fact, she said, always, that she could see a little better.

At the end of the consultation the eye-doctor wrapped up a bottle of lotion in white paper and Osborn paid the seven and six. Osborn felt that by doing so he paid for something else besides a cure. He bought prestige, importance, some essence of slight mystery, a thing to boast about.

"Cost us pounds a'ready. Every week she's got 'ev this special tackle. You can't git it in England. He gits it from India — it's some rare herb or summat and it don't grow in England. Gits it from some head man over there. Ah. I tell y', costs us pounds, costs us a small fortune. You know what he told me? Reckons where he comes from they ain't got such things as bad eyes and like o' that. It's this herb as does it."

Then one week the girl could read only the large capitals on the text-cards. At home the hens had begun to resemble balls of brown and white mist. With the mist closing down on her, she was more frightened than ever.

"Well, I think it may be only temporary.

But just to be on the safe side, I am going to give you a new lotion." The voice was easy, smooth, like a beautiful oil itself. "Now Mr. Osborn, I should charge you one pound for this lotion. The herb from which it is distilled is very rare indeed and in my country it only grows on hills above 10,000 feet, and it can only be gathered after the snow has melted. My people have known about it for centuries. You see? But wait please — wait one moment, please, one moment. I am not going to charge you one pound, not anything like one pound. Because I know you, because I want your daughter to get better — half price. To you only, half-price. Ten shillings."

"Half a quid a week — that's what it costs us. Enough to break anybody — but there y'are. I don't care what it costs, I ain't goin' t'ave anybody say I was too mean to fork out the dough. Course, he ain't ordinary doctor — you don't expect to pay ordinary prices."

One morning it was not the eye-doctor but a woman who opened the

234

door, and the card was not in the window.

"No, he ain't come."

"Very like had a break-down? — puncture or summat?"

"Well, it seems funny. He always drops me a card so as I get it first post Tuesdays. But to-day I ain't had one."

"H'm, funny. Well, we'll go back to market and then come round again."

At twelve and again in the afternoon Mr. Varipatana was not there. They drove home. "Hope he ain't bad or nothing. You're sure he must be took bad or else he'd write?" They spoke with concern, making the illness of an important man a thing of importance for themselves.

To the girl it seemed as if they drove in semi-darkness. She could hear the wind, now, with the aggravated keenness of her hearing, as she had never heard it in her life. Her mind gathered the sounds and translated them into images. The sounds seemed to her to come through an immense expanse of space. She sat with her hands in her lap and when she touched one hand against another she was reminded of the sensation of Mr. Varipatana's hands pressing on her eyes. They seemed to be pressing her down into greater darkness.

"Well, I hope nothing's happened to the man. I hope he ain't been took bad or nothing. She's used every drop o' lotion up."

They drove down to market as usual, a week later. Mr. Varipatana was not there.

"He ain't bad?"

"I dunno. He sent a letter saying he wasn't comin' no more. That's all I know."

In the afternoon they drove back, the eyes of the man and woman depressed, short-focused, as though seeing nothing, the girl with her eyes still and fixed, as though on some illimitable distance. Osborn felt cheated, turning the lost money over and over in his mind.

The girl sat with her hands in her lap. She recalled the touch of Mr. Varipatana's hands on her eyelids, and it seemed suddenly as if the hands shut down the lids with suave finality, for ever.

The car stopped before she was aware of it. She was jerked back to reality. She felt the pressure of mist on her eyes and was frightened.

Instinctively she put out her hands.

Shot Actress — Full Story

THERE were fifteen thousand people in Claypole, but only one actress. She kept a milliner's shop.

My name is Sprake. I kept the watchmaker-and-jeweller's shop next door to Miss Porteus for fifteen years. During all that time she never spoke to me. I am not sure that she ever spoke to anyone; I never saw her. My wife and I were a decent, respectable devoted couple, Wesleyans, not above speaking to anyone, and I have been on the local stage myself, singing in oratorio, but we were never good enough for Miss Porteus. But that was her affair. If she hadn't been so standoffish she might, perhaps, have been alive to-day. As it is she is dead and she died, as everybody knows, on the front page of the newspapers.

No one in Claypole knew much about Miss Porteus. We knew she had been an actress, but where she had been an actress, and in what plays and in what theatres, and when, nobody knew. She looked like an actress: she was tall and very haughty and her hair, once blonde, was something of the colour of tobacco-stained moustaches, a queer yellowish ginger, as though the dye had gone wrong. Her lips were red and bitter; and with her haughty face she looked like a cold nasty woman in a play. She dressed, just for show, exactly the opposite of every other woman in Claypole: in winter she came out in chiffon and in summer you would see her walking across the golf-course, not speaking to anyone, in great fox furs something the colour of her own hair.

Her shop was just the same: at a time when every milliner-draper in Claypole used to cram as much into the shop-window as possible, Miss Porteus introduced that style of one hat on a stand and a vase of expensive flowers on a length of velvet. But somehow that never quite came off. The solitary hat looked rather like Miss Porteus herself: lonely and haughty and out of place.

The backways of her shop and ours

faced on to each other; the gardens were divided by a partition of boards and fencing, but we could see from our bathroom into Miss Porteus's bathroom. You could see a great array of fancy cosmetic bottles outlined behind the frosted glass. You could see Miss Porteus at her toilet. But you never saw anyone else there.

Then one day we did see someone else there. One Wednesday morning my wife came scuffling into the shop and behind the counter, where I was mending a tuppenny-ha'penny Swiss lever that I'd had lying about for months, and said that she'd seen a man in Miss Porteus's back-yard.

"Well, what about it?" I said. "I don't care if there's fifty men. Perhaps that's what she wants, a man or two," I said. Just like that.

I was busy and I thought no more about it. But as it turned out afterwards, my wife did. I daresay she was a bit inquisitive, but while she was arranging the bedroom curtains she saw the man several times. She got a clear view of him: he was middle-aged and he had side-linings and he wore a yellow tie.

That night, when I went to bed, the light was burning in Miss Porteus's bathroom, but I couldn't see Miss Porteus. Then when I went into the bathroom next morning the light was still burning. I said, "Hullo, Miss Porteus left the light on all night," but I thought no more about it. Then when I went up at midday, the light was still on. It was still on that afternoon and it was on all that night.

My wife was scared. But I said, "Oh! it's Thursday and she's taken a day off and gone up to London." But the light went on burning all the next day and it was still burning late that night.

By that time I was puzzled myself. I went and tried Miss Porteus's shop door. It was locked. But there was really nothing strange about that. It was eleven o'clock at night and it ought to have been locked.

We went to bed, but my wife couldn't sleep. She kept saying I ought to do something. "What can I do?" I said. At last she jumped up in bed. "You've got to get a ladder out and climb up and see if everything's all right in Miss Porteus's bathroom," she said.

"Oh! all right," I said.

So I heaved our ladder over the boards and then ran it up to Miss Porteus's bathroom window. I climbed up. That was the picture they took of me later on: up the ladder, pointing to the bathroom window, which was marked with a cross. All the papers had it in.

What I saw through the bathroom window, even through the frosted glass, was bad enough, but it was only when I had telephoned to the police station and we had forced an entrance that I saw how really terrible it was.

Miss Porteus was lying on the bathroom floor with a bullet wound in her chest. We banged the door against her head as we went in. She had been dead for some time and I could almost calculate how long, because of the light. She was in a cerise pink nightgown and the blood had made a little rosette on her chest.

"Bolt the garden gate and say nothing to nobody," the sergeant said.

I said nothing. The next morning all Claypole knew that Miss Porteus had been murdered, and by afternoon the whole of England knew. The reporter from the *Argus*, the local paper, came rushing round to see me before seven o'clock. "Give me it," he said. "Give me it before they get here. I'm on lineage for the *Express* and I'll rush it through. Just the bare facts. What you saw. I'll write it." So I made a statement. It was just a plain statement, and every word of it was true.

Then just before dinner I saw three men with cameras on the opposite side of the street. They took pictures of Miss Porteus's shop, and then they came across the road into my shop. They as good as forced their way through the shop, into the backyard, and there they photographed Miss Porteus's bathroom window. Then one of the cameramen put a pound note into my hand and said, "On top of the ladder?" The ladder was still there and I climbed up and they photographed me on top of it, pointing at the window.

By afternoon the crowd was packed thick right across the street. They were pressed tight against my window. I put the shutters up. Just as I was finishing them, four men came up and said they were newspaper-men and could I give them the facts about Miss Porteus?

Before I could speak they pushed into the shop. They shut the door. Then I saw that there were not four of them but twelve. I got behind the counter and they took out notebooks and rested them on my glass show-cases and scribbled. I tried to tell them what I had told the local man, the truth, and nothing more or less than the truth, but they didn't want that. They hammered me with questions.

What was Miss Porteus like? Was her real name Porteus? What else beside Porteus? What colour was her hair? How long had she been there? Did it strike me as funny that an actress should run a milliner's shop? When had I last seen the lady? About the bathroom — about her hair —

I was flustered and I said something about her hair being a little reddish, and one of the newspaper men said:

"Now we're getting somewhere. Carrots," and they all laughed.

Then another said: "Everybody says

this woman was an actress. But where did she act? London? What theatre? When?"

"I don't know," I said.

"You've lived next door all this time and don't know? Did you never hear anybody say if she'd been in any particular play?"

"No. I — Well, she was a bit strange."

"Strange?" They seized on that. "How? What? Mysterious?"

"Well," I said, "she was the sort of woman who'd come out in big heavy fox furs on a hot summer day. She was different."

"Crazy?"

"Oh! No."

"Eccentric?"

"No. I wouldn't say that."

"About her acting," they said. "You must have heard something."

"No." Then I remembered something. At a rehearsal of the Choral Society, once, her name had come up and somebody had said something about her having been in *Othello*. I remembered it because there was some argument about whether Othello was a pure black or just a half-caste.

"Othello?" The newspaper-men wrote fast. "What was she? Desdemona?"

"Well," I said. "I don't think you ought to put that in. I don't know if it's strictly true or not. I can't vouch for it. I don't think — "

"And this man that was seen," they said. "When was it? When did you see him? What was he like?"

I said I didn't know, that I hadn't seen him, but that my wife had. So they had my wife in. They questioned her. They were nice to her. But they put down, as in my case, things she did not say. Yellow tie? Dark? How dark? Foreign-looking? Actor? Every now and then one of them dashed out to the post office. They questioned us all that afternoon.

The next morning the placards of the morning newspapers were all over Claypole. "Shot Actress — Full Story." It was my story, but somehow, as it appeared in the papers, it was not true. I read all the papers. They had my picture, the picture of Miss Porteus's shop, looking somehow strange and forlorn with its drawn blind, and a picture of

246

Miss Porteus herself, as she must have looked about 1920. All over these papers were black stabbing headlines: 'Search for Shot Actress Assailant Goes On.' 'Police anxious to Interview Foreigner with Yellow Tie.' 'Real Life Desdemona: Jealousy Victim?' 'Eccentric Actress Recluse Dead in Bathroom.' 'Mystery Life of Actress who wore Furs in Heat Wave.' 'Beautiful Red-haired Actress who Spoke to Nobody.' 'Disappearance of Dark-looking Foreigner.'

It was Saturday. That afternoon Claypole was besieged by hundreds of people who had never been there before. They moved past Miss Porteus's shop and mine in a great stream, in cars and on foot and pushing bicycles, staring up at the dead actress's windows. They climbed in over the fence of my back-garden and trampled on the flower-beds, until the police stopped them. Towards evening the crowd was so thick outside, in the front, that I put the shutters up again, and by six o'clock I closed the shop. The police kept moving the crowd on, but it was no use. It swarmed out of the High Street into the side street and then round by the back streets until it came into High Street again. Hundreds of people who had seen Miss Porteus's shop every day of their lives suddenly wanted to stare at it. They came to stare at the sun-faded blinds, just like any other shop blinds, as though they were jewelled; they fought to get a glimpse of the frosted pane of Miss Porteus's bathroom. All the tea shops in Claypole that day were crowded out.

We had reporters and photographers and detectives tramping about the house and the garden all that day and the next. That Sunday morning I missed going to chapel, where I used to sing tenor in the choir, for the first time for almost ten years. My wife could not sleep and she was nervously exhausted and kept crying. The Sunday newspapers were full of it again: the pictures of poor Miss Porteus, the shop, the bathroom window, my shop, the headlines. That afternoon the crowds began again, thicker than ever, and all the tea shops which normally did not open on Sunday opened and were packed out. A man started to sell souvenir photographs of Claypole High Street in the streets at threepence each, and it was as though he were selling pound notes or bits of Miss Porteus's hair. The sweet-shops opened and you saw people buying Claypole rock and Claypole treacle toffee, which is a speciality of the town. The police drafted in extra men and right up to ten o'clock strange people kept going by, whole families, with children, in their Sunday clothes, staring up at Miss Porteus's windows, with mouths open.

That afternoon I went for a walk, just for a few minutes, to get some air. Everybody I knew stopped me and wanted to talk, and one man I knew only slightly stopped me and said, "What she look like, in the nightgown? See anything?" Another said: "Ah, you don't tell me she lived there all alone for nothing. I know one man who knew his way upstairs. And where there's one you may depend there's others. She knew her way about."

The inquest was held on the Monday. It lasted three days. My wife and I were witnesses and it came out, then, that Miss Porteus's name was not Porteus at all, but Helen Williams. Porteus had been her stage name. It came out also that there was a conflict of opinion in the medical evidence, that it was not clear if Miss Porteus had been murdered or if she had taken her life. It was a very curious, baffling case, made more complicated because the man with the yellow tie had not been found, and the jury returned an open verdict.

All this made it much worse. The fact of Miss Porteus having had two names gave her an air of mystery, of duplicity, and the doubts about her death increased it. There sprang up, gradually, a different story about Miss Porteus. It began to go all over Claypole that she was a woman of a certain reputation, that the milliner's shop was a blind. "Did you ever see anybody in there, or going in? No, nor did anybody else. Did anybody ever buy a hat there? No. But the back door was always undone." That rumour gave cause for others. "Sprake," people began to say, "told me himself that she lay on the floor naked. They put the nightgown on afterwards." Then she became not only a woman of light virtue and naked, but also pregnant. "That's why," people began to say, "she either shot herself or was shot. Take it which way you like. But I had it straight from Sprake."

As the story of Miss Porteus grew, the story of my own part in it grew. Business had been very bad and for three days, because of the inquest, I had had to close the shop, but suddenly people began to come in. They looked out old watches and clocks that needed repairing, brooches that had been out of fashion for years and needed remodelling, and they brought them in; they came in to buy watches, knick-knacks, ash-trays, bits of jewellery, clocks, anything. A man asked for an ash-tray with Claypole church on it as a souvenir.

By the week-end I was selling all the souvenirs I could lay hands on. The shop was never empty. I took my meals standing up and by the end of the day my wife and I were worn out by that extraordinary mad rush of business. We rested in bed all day on Sunday, exhausted. Then on Monday it all began again, not quite so bad, but almost. We were besieged by people coming in, ostensibly to buy something, but in

251

reality on the chance of hearing me say something about Miss Porteus's death. I was in a dilemma: I wanted to close the shop and end it all, but somehow it wasn't possible. Business is business and death is death and you've got to live. And so I kept open.

Then the police came to see me again. The man with the yellow tie had not been found and they wanted my wife and me to go to the station to check the statements we had given. We shut the shop and drove to the station in a taxi. We were there three hours. When we got back there was a crowd of fifty people round the shop, murmuring and pushing and arguing among themselves. The rumour had gone round that the police had arrested me.

Once that rumour had begun, nothing could stop its consequences. It was a rumour that never quite became tangible. It drifted about like smoke. It was there, but you could never grasp it. No one would really say anything, but the rumour was all over Claypole that I knew more than I would say. With one rumour went others: it began to be said that my wife

252

and I were busybodies, Nosy-Parkers. How else had we come to be squinting into Miss Porteus's bathroom? How else had we seen the man with the yellow tie in the back-yard? We were Peeping-Toms. I never heard anyone say this. But it was there. I saw it in people's faces: I felt it. I felt it as plainly as a man feels the change of weather in an old wound.

But there was one thing I did hear them say. I used to belong, in Claypole, to a Temperance Club, the Melrose; we had four full-sized billiard tables and in the evenings I went there to play billiards and cards, to have a smoke and a talk and so on. Next to the billiard-room was a small cloak-room, and one evening, as I was hanging up my coat, I heard someone at the billiard table say:

"Old Sprake knows a thing or two. Think I should be here if I had as many quid as times old Sprake's been upstairs next door? Actress, my eye. Some act. Pound a time. Ever struck you it was funny old Sprake knew the colour of that nightgown so well?"

I put on my coat again and went out of the club. I was trembling and horrified and sick. What I had heard seemed to be the crystallization of all the rumours that perhaps were and perhaps were not going round Claypole. It may have been simply the crystallization of my own fears. I don't know. I only know that I felt that I was suspected of things I had not done and had not said; that not only was Miss Porteus a loose woman but that I had had illicit relations with her; that not only was she pregnant but that I, perhaps, had had something to do with that pregnancy; that not only had she been murdered, but that I knew more than I would say about that murder. I was harassed by fears and counter fears. I did not know what to do.

And all the time that mad rush of customers went on. All day people would be coming in to buy things they did not want, just on the off-chance of hearing me say something about Miss Porteus's death, or of asking me some questions about her life. It was so tiring and irritating that I had to defend myself from it. So I hit upon the idea of saying the same thing to everybody.

"I just don't know," I would say. I said

it to everyone. Just that: "I just don't know."

I suppose I must have said those words hundreds of times a day. I suppose I often said them whether they were necessary or not. And when a man goes on repeating one sentence hundreds of times a day, for two or three weeks, it is only natural, perhaps, that people should begin to wonder about his sanity.

So it crept round Claypole that I was a little queer. One day I had to go to London on business and a man in the same compartment as myself said to another: "Take any murder you like. It's always the work of somebody half-sharp, a maniac. Take that Claypole murder. Clear as daylight. The work of somebody loopy."

That was not directed against me, but it stirred up my fears into a great ugly, lumpy mass of doubt and terror. I could not sleep. And when I looked into the glass, after a restless night, I saw a face made queer and wretched by the strain of unresolved anxieties. I felt that I could have broken down, in the middle of that rush of customers and questions and fears and rumours, and wept like a child.

Then something happened. It was important and it suddenly filled the front pages of the newspapers again with the mystery of Miss Porteus's death. The police found the man with the yellow tie. It was a sensation.

The man was a theatrical producer named Prideaux and the police found him at Brighton. The fact that his name was French and that he was found at Brighton at once established him, in the public mind, as the murderer of Miss Porteus.

But he had an explanation. He had not come forward because, quite naturally, he was afraid. Miss Porteus was an old friend and her death, he said, had upset him terribly. It was true that he had seen Miss Porteus just before her death, because Miss Porteus had invited him to come and see her. She needed money; the millinery business was not paying its way. She feared bankruptcy and, according to Prideaux, had threatened to take her life. Prideaux promised to lend her some money and he was back in London early that evening. He proved it. The porter of his hotel could prove it. It was also proved that people had seen Miss Porteus, alive, walking out on the golf-course, as late as five o'clock that day. The hotel-porter could prove that Prideaux was in London by that time.

That was the end. It was established, beyond doubt, that Miss Porteus had taken her life. And suddenly all the mystery and sensation and horror and fascination of Miss Porteus's death became nothing. The papers were not interested in her any longer and her name has never appeared in the papers again.

I no longer live at Claypole. All those odd, unrealized rumours that went round were enough to drive me mad; but they were also enough to kill my wife. Like me, she could not sleep, and the shock of it all cracked her life right across, like a piece of bone. Rumour and shock and worry killed her, and she died just after the facts of Miss Porteus's death were established. A month later I gave up the business and left the town. I could not go on. The first week before her death I had three people in the shop. All that mad inquisitiveness had hardened into indifference. Nobody wanted anything any longer. Nobody even stopped to stare up at Miss Porteus's windows.

Poor Miss Porteus. She took her life because she was hard up, in a fit of despair. There is no more to it than that. But nobody in Claypole ever believed that and I suppose very few people ever will. In Claypole they like to think that she was murdered; they know, because the papers said so, that she was a strange and eccentric woman; they know that she acted in a play with a black man; they know, though nobody ever really said so, that she was a loose woman and that she was pregnant and that somebody shot her for that reason; they know that she let men in and up the back stairs at a pound a time and they like to think that I was one of those men; they know that I found her naked in the bathroom and that I was a bit queer and that I knew more than I would ever say.

They know, in short, all that happened to Miss Porteus. They can never know how much has happened to me.

The Dog and Mr. Morency

MR. ALEXANDER MORENCY, residing at Seaview Hotel, the Esplanade, had a little dog, Fritz, a Pomeranian. Mr. Morency came to a decision to shoot either the dog or Mrs. Morency. He could not make up his mind.

Curiously, Mr. Morency had first wanted the dog. This had been in the days when the Morencys lived at 'Morency', 3 Lilac Gardens, close to Regent's Park, and Mr. Morency was in business as a tea-broker, in the City. Mrs. Morency had not then wanted a dog. "Me? A dog? What should I do with a dog?" she would say. "All over the furniture, paddling in and out in wet weather. Besides, there's some other things I don't like about them." Morency, a small, easy-going gentle fellow with a voice like smooth toffee, who wore rimless glasses, tried to persuade her otherwise. "You see you're alone here all day, and

259

that isn't good for you. One hears stories of fellows calling ostensibly to sell floor polish and well — You need company, and you can't have better company than a dog. Everybody knows that, and it will protect you as well."

Mr. Morency had not at that time considered the question of breed, but he had in his mind the idea of a large dog, some kind of mastiff. He saw himself exercising this mastiff in the park on Sunday mornings, and felt the power of it on the leash, of the great neck straining magnificently forward, the muscles rippling silkily, hard as rubber. He wanted a dog that was a dog, a fighting dog, a dog that if necessary might have to be muzzled. He felt vaguely some latent power in himself expressed in the thought of such a dog.

"Well, if I must have a dog," Mrs. Morency said at last, "I'll have a Pomeranian."

"Oh! no. Have a dog. Have a dog that you can call a dog."

"Well, isn't a Pomeranian a dog? What's wrong with a Pomeranian?"

"In the first place," Mr. Morency said,

"it's a dog of German origin. And we can do without German dogs, I think. Then the whole idea of your having a dog at all is for you to have protection."

"You said companionship."

"Well, if you like. Companionship as well if you like. But primarily protection. Because you're alone in the house. Now if you would make up your mind on some dog like an Alsatian — "

"Oh! no. Beastly things. I can't bear them."

"Well, all right. A Labrador."

"What's a Labrador?"

So Mr. Morency explained what a Labrador was, but Mrs. Morency was not impressed. Then he described a Collie, and then a Sheep Dog, subsequently other large dogs, including a Wolfhound. He even went so far as to describe a St. Bernard. He became very enthusiastic about a St. Bernard, playing on Mrs. Morency's maternal instincts. Mr. and Mrs. Morency had had no children and Mr. Morency kept saying didn't Mrs. Morency know that it was the St. Bernard who, with brandy flask, rescued lost snow-bound little children from death in Alpine passes?

But Mrs. Morency merely pointed out that St. Bernards ate a lot.

"Well, yes," Mr. Morency said, "admitted. A lot for their size yes. But — "

"I don't want a dog that eats a lot."

"Well, have a Collie. They don't eat so much."

"And I don't want a dog that needs a kennel. If I'm going to have a dog I'll have a dog that'll be easy to keep, and that can come into the house and eat with us."

"Yes, but the whole idea — "

"I'll have a Pomeranian," Mrs. Morency said.

"Oh! no. Please."

"I'll have a Pomeranian," Mrs. Morency said, "and I'll call him Fritz."

When the Pomeranian arrived Mr. Morency almost liked it. It was soft and odd and puppy-playful, and he would roll it into a little black woollen ball in his hands. It wetted the cushions, but Mrs. Morency said that was natural, wasn't it? and Mr. Morency forgave it when it rolled in the geraniums. Mrs. Morency called it Fritzie, and bought a dog basket and lined the basket with red silk. The dog slept in the box-room and for a night or two was frightened, whimpering, and Mrs. Morency woke up and put on her dressing-gown and went to comfort it. Another day Mrs. Morency was wildly excited when Mr. Morency came home. "It drinks tea! I gave it tea in a saucer and it drank it! Tea! There's a knowing creature for you. You a tea-broker and it drinks tea! Couldn't you bring it home a little caddy with some nice special Darjeeling in it, all its own?"

Mr. Morency brought home a little half-pound caddy, filled with Darjeeling, and Mrs. Morency wrote a label on it — 'Fritz'. Then Sunday came and Mrs. Morency said, "Dogs need exercise. Would you like to take Fritzie for an hour into the park?"

With great reluctance Mr. Morency took the dog into the park. There were a great many dogs in the park. It seemed to him that there were, that morning, unusually large numbers of large dogs. He saw Alsatians with wild cocked ears, big Collies, vast Labradors bounding after balls across the grass. Fritzie strained at the leash and Mr. Morency strained back, walking almost on his heels, trying to foster the illusion of power. But it was no good: he could not blind himself to the reality of the little Pomeranian, miserable and despicable, so absurd that it did not even know what a tree was for. And he felt that he was on the verge of hating it.

But it was not until some time afterwards that he felt his hatred become a reality. In the autumn of that year Mr. Morency retired from business, and the Morencys decided to go and live at the seaside.

"Of course," Mr. Morency said, "we shall have to get rid of Fritz."

"Get what? What do you mean? Get rid of Fritz?"

"Why, yes. You can't take a dog to live in an hotel. No hotel will have it."

"Oh! won't they? We'll see about that. We'll find an hotel that does."

Mrs. Morency went to several hotels and even took Fritz down to them, to see the managers. Finally the Seaview Hotel said it did not mind little dogs, providing they were well-trained.

"He has his own bed and bath and even his own tea-caddy. Oh! yes, and he even has other necessary things too. He's an angel."

So the Morency's moved into the Seaview Hotel, and every morning, before breakfast, and every evening, after supper, Mr. Morency exercised the Pomeranian along the Esplanade with the sea-wind in his face. Mr. Morency tried hard to foster the old illusion of grappling with a powerful animal. But it was no good: he saw only the wretched yelping and yapping little Fritz, who would never grow any bigger.

And in the hotel lounge, every day, the Pomeranian did his tricks. "Fritzie sit up! up! Up! Steady, Fritzie, wait. Fritzie, wait. Naughty Fritzie. Fritzie wait, wait. Now — catch it!" And Fritzie would catch the biscuit. "Now," Mrs. Morency would say, "cow jump over the moon." And Mrs. Morency would hold up a saucer and call to Fritzie: "Cow jump over the moon! Fritzie, now, Fritzie cow jump — Fritzie, naughty Fritzie. Naughty Fritzie not looking. Now. Cow jumps over — Fritzie, Fritzie. Naughty.

No jump, no cakey. Now cow — steady — cow jumps over the moon!"

And the ladies in the lounge would say what a wonderful little thing Fritzie was.

"Oh! yes. He's so knowing. He knows it's teatime when I rattle a spoon in a cup, and he knows it's walkie time, don't you Fritzie?, if I just pick up his lead. And he knows — well, he can *tell* me when he — "

And hearing the voice of Mrs. Morency praising and explaining the dog and seeing the dog itself, paws up, begging for biscuit day after day in the hotel lounge, Mr. Morency felt the gradual growth and hardening of a peculiar hatred towards them both. He saw himself for the rest of his life exercising the dog morning and evening, getting out of bed to give it its saucer of early morning tea, hearing its silly yappings of joy and misery, smelling the old dog-smell about the room. He began to long for the day when the dog would get run over by a bus, and in desperation, once or twice, he called it suddenly across the road on the off-chance that it would get run over by the bus. He felt jealous of the dog because of his wife's affection for it, jealous of his wife because of the dog's everlasting yapping and stupid affection for her. He hated the walk along the Esplanade, and he could not sleep at night, the thought of the dog boring into his mind like a gimblet. Until finally he felt he could bear it no longer.

He decided to shoot the dog. He would take it down on the sea shore, one dark evening, and shoot it and let the tide wash it away. If there was any trouble afterwards, he would probably shoot Mrs. Morency too.

And one evening, after dinner, he took the dog far along the Esplanade. He had an old service revolver in his overcoat pocket and he would shoot the dog down under the cliffs, where the lamps ended. As he walked along he passed other men exercising other dogs, and suddenly, instead of being remorseful, he was struck by the whole outrageous idea of dogs on earth. He thought of all the dogs being exercised, for the same purpose, along that piece of sea-front, and then of all the dogs being exercised, still for the same purpose, along all the sea-fronts of England. He thought of the thousands of dogs all over England, and then of the millions of dogs all over Europe, and all the other millions of dogs from China to San Francisco, from Greenland to Honolulu. There were millions of dogs in the world and what were they worth? You couldn't milk them, you couldn't eat them and sometimes, he felt bitterly, you couldn't trust them. They were pampered parasites, an outrage, and nobody saw it. They didn't even hunt their own food, like cats, and he saw all the vast unharnessed power of dog muscle all over the world as something which was worth nothing at all.

He tugged the Pomeranian down to the shore. In the half-darkness he could just see it: miserable, despicable, an absolute caricature of a dog. He thought of the dog he had wanted, the mastiff. He felt the tremendous pull of it on the sockets of his arms, the strength of a dog that was a dog.

He got the Pomeranian by the collar with his left hand and held it down against the still sea-wet shingle. Below him he could hear the tide going out, washing the pebbles. There was no other sound except the wind up on the cliffs. The dog was making no sound at all.

As Mr. Morency looked at it, there was just a faint light from the last lamp on the Esplanade, and unexpectedly Mr. Morency saw the dog's eyes. He looked at them and suddenly, for about a second, he saw in the reflecting eyes of the small dog a small reflection of himself. He saw the dim light of something abject, downtrodden, a little forlorn, deeply unhappy.

And in that moment he could have shot himself.

The Wreath

THE train was almost ready to start when the old man and the girl came into the carriage. The girl was very sweet with him, putting his travelling case and the wreath on the rack, reminding him of things, kissing him very tenderly good-bye.

"You know where you're going? Now don't forget. Ham Street. First stop and then you change and get the other train. You think you'll remember? Ham Street and change first stop?"

"Yes. I think I shall remember."

"And carry the wreath this way up. Like this. You see, there's a little handle."

He said yes, he would remember and carry it that way up, and then she kissed him good-bye through the open window and the train moved away.

"Oh! dear," he said to me, "we went to the wrong station and then had to run for it."

He was dressed all in black. He had

270

pure white hair and a very pink fresh face, and he looked rather like a picture of a French priest. He gave me a smile. "When you get over eighty, running for trains isn't what it used to be."

"You're not over eighty?" I said.

"Oh! yes. Eighty-three. You think I don't look it?"

He looked perhaps seventy. I said so.

"They all say that," he said. "No, eighty-three. At eighty I had an illness, a sort of stroke, and the doctors said, 'You won't get better.' Then I did get better and they said, 'it's very remarkable. We'll give lectures on you,' and so they've been giving lectures on me." He looked up at the rack. "is the wreath all right?"

"Yes," I said, "it's all right."

He was silent and I thought perhaps he was tired of talking and I handed him an evening paper.

"No," he said, "thank you. Thank you all the same. But since my illness I can't read. I can write, but I can't read." He looked out of the window at the darkness. "Yes," he said, "Yes."

He looked at me. "What were we talking about?"

271

"You were telling me," I said, "how you could write but not read."

"Ah yes. Yes." He began to forage in his pockets. "Yes, I can write. I write quite well, quite straight." He turned out first one pocket and then another. "I am trying to find a specimen of my writing." He found a piece of blue paper. "No. That's who I am, where I'm travelling to. In case I get lost."

He gave me the paper to read. it had written on it: "Simpson. Travelling to Ham Street."

"I am going to a funeral," he said. "Is the wreath all right?"

"Yes," I said, "it's all right."

He took out his snuff-box, opened it and handed it to me. I thanked him and said no. The box was silver and on the lid were engraved figures of men cycling. He said, "The arms of my cycling club. I do a great deal of cycling."

"Still?"

"Oh, yes! In the summer. Oh yes! I cycle all over the countryside."

Again he looked out of the window, briefly, watching the darkness. Then he looked at me.

272

"What were we talking about?"

"About the cycling."

"Ah yes. Yes. About the cycling. Oh! yes I'm energetic. I go into the bathroom every morning and wash in cold water and do my exercises. Take a bath once a week. Cycle in summer."

He held out his hands to me.

"Are they the hands of a man of eighty-three?"

They were full, beautiful hands, wonderfully pink and fresh like his face.

"Oh, no!" he said. "In summer I cycle from Ham Street to Rye, three times a week, to get a shave."

"That's a long way."

"Seven miles."

For a time he told me about the cycling. Then he began to tell me about his youth.

"I was a grocer. An apprentice." He stopped. "But this is not fair to you. Talking about myself."

"I like it," I said.

"You have some way of making me do it," he said. He paused, looked up. "The wreath is all right?"

"Yes, it's all right. I'll watch it."

"What were we talking about?"

I told him.

"Oh, yes. We sold everything. Provisions, furniture, blankets, stockings. A big connection. I used to drive about the country in a trap, taking orders. Ladies' stockings. Oh, yes! In those days you measured the length of the leg. Pleasant. Blankets was another thing. I remember selling a hundred pairs of blankets in one day, just by telling them that I'd dreamed it was going to be the coldest winter on record."

"And now," I said, "it's all different?"

"Oh, yes!"

"You sit back and take it easy?"

"Oh, no! I'm the director of a company with a capital of five million." He put his hand on his neck-tie. "You see that pin?"

"The Prince of Wales's feathers?"

"Exactly. The late Edward VII gave it to me. Any time I like I can walk into Buckingham Palace."

The train was rushing on. The wreath trembled as we swayed over points.

"What was I saying?"

I reminded him. He went on to talk

274

about his daughter. "She is a pianist. You may have heard of her?" He told me her name. I said yes, I had heard of her.

"You are musical yourself?" he said.

"Yes."

"I knew it. You have a musical face."

I told him how I heard his daughter, often, play the piano. He was touched. The train rushed on, lights were hurled past us in the darkness. Sitting silent, he suddenly looked frail and tender. I thought of him as a boy, measuring the ladies' legs for stockings, in the seventies. He took out his snuff-box.

"You really won't try any?"

I hesitated.

"Go on."

"All right."

"Snuff said!" he laughed.

We took snuff together, holding the pinches delicately in our hands, his own strong and pink, the sniff of his nostrils urgent and deep.

"I shan't forget you," he said. "I keep a diary. I shall put you in it."

We sat silent. I felt suddenly very close to him, as though I had known him a long time. He looked out of the window, at the travelling blackness, then at me again.

"Where am I going?" he said, like a child.

"To Ham Street. Don't you remember?" I said.

"Oh, yes! I remember."

We talked a little more, I blew the snuff down my nose, and then I saw lights flashing past, increasing, in the darkness, and the train began to slow down.

I got up. "I'll get the wreath down for you," I said.

I reached up and got down the wreath and the suit-case. I held the wreath by the little handle of string looped at one end. "I'll carry it and find out about your train," I said.

"It's very nice of you."

When the train stopped at the junction we got out and I found out about his train and then took him to where it was waiting, in the opposite platform. He got into the carriage and I followed him and settled his things for him, putting the wreath on the rack above his head.

"You know where you're going?" I said.

"Yes. I haven't forgotten."

We said good-bye and shook hands and slowly, in a little while, the train moved off. He waved his beautiful pink hands out of the window and the wreath trembled above his head.

Elephant's Nest in a Rhubarb Tree

THE summer I had the scarlet fever the only boy I could play with, during and after the scarlet fever, was Arty Whitehead. Arty had some buttons off and he lived with his uncle. His uncle had an elephant's nest in a rhubarb tree.

It was very hot that summer. As I leaned from the bedroom window and looked down on the street of new brick houses and waited for Arty to come and play with me the window-sill would scorch my elbows like hot sand-paper. On the wall of our house my father had planted a Virginia creeper. That summer, under the heat, it went mad. It pressed new shoots forward every day and they ran over the house and the house next door and then the house on the corner like bright green and wine-red lizards with tiny hands. One of the games I played was to watch how far the creeper grew in a week, sometimes how far it grew in a day. After three or four weeks it grew round the corner of the street and I could no longer see the new little lizards glueing their hands on the wall. So I would send Arty round the corner to look instead. "How far's it grown now, Arty?" Arty would stand by the green railings of our house and look up. He had simple, tender eyes and his hair grew down in his neck and over his ears and he always talked with a smile, loosely. "Growed right up to mother Kingsley's! Yeh, yeh! Growed up to the shop," he'd say. Mother Kingsley's was a hundred yards up the next street. But I was only six, I couldn't see round the corner, and either I had to believe in Arty or believe in nobody. And gradually, as the summer went on, I got into the way of believing in Arty.

Arty came to play with me every day. Another game I played was blowing soap bubbles with a clay pipe. They floated down from the open window and Arty ran about the street, trying to catch them with his hands. One day I blew a bubble as big as a melon, the biggest bubble I'd ever seen, the biggest bubble that anyone would ever have seen if there'd been anyone in the street to see it. But there was no one but Arty. This great melon bubble floated slowly down in the hot sunshine and then along the scorched empty street. The funny thing about it was that it wouldn't burst. It floated beautifully away like a glass balloon polished by sun, keeping about as high as the windows of the houses. When it got to the street-corner a puff of wind caught it and it turned the corner and disappeared. I called to Arty to run after it and he ran like mad after it with his cap in his hand. It was then about two o'clock in the afternoon but Arty didn't come back until six that evening.

When he came back again his lips were tired and looser than ever and I could see that he'd been a long way. "Where you been?" I said.

"Arter the balloon."

"All this time? Didn't it bust?" I said.

"No," he said, "it never busted. Just kept like that. Just went on. Never busted."

"Where?" I said. "How far?"

"Went right up past the school and over Collins's pond and over the fields. Right out to Newton. Past our farm."

"Whose farm?"

"Our farm. Went right over. Never busted."

"I never knew you had a farm," I said.

"Yeh, yeh," Arty said. "My uncle gotta farm. Big farm."

"Where?"

"Out there," Arty said. "Just out there. Great big farm. Catch foxes. Catch wild animals."

"What wild animals?"

"Foxes. All sorts," Arty said. "All sorts. Elephants."

"Not elephants," I said.

"Yeh, yeh," Arty said. "Yeh! Catch elephants. My uncle found elephant's nest one day." His eyes were pale and excited. "Yeh! Elephant's nest in a rhubarb tree."

That was the first I ever heard about it. In the beginning I had to believe Arty about the Virginia creeper, then I had to take his word for the bubble, which no one but Arty and I had ever seen. Then I did something else. Perhaps it was the after effects of the fever, the result of being shut up for nearly eight weeks in a bedroom which was almost like a boiler-house in the late afternoons; perhaps it was because I had temporarily forgotten what the world of reality, school and fields and sweetshops and trains, was like. Perhaps it was having Arty to talk to, and only Arty to play with. But gradually, from that day, I began to take his word too for the elephant's nest in a rhubarb tree.

After that, I began to ask him to tell me what it was like, but he never gave me the same description twice. "Yeh," he would say. "It's big. Ever so big. Big rhubarb." And then another day it was different. "It's jus' a little squatty tree. Nest like a sparrow's. That's all. Little squatty tree." Finally I was not sure what to believe in: whether the rhubarb tree was like a chestnut or an oak, with a nest of elephants like a haystack in the branches, or whether it was just rhubarb, just ordinary rhubarb, the rhubarb you eat, and it was a nest like a sparrow's, with little elephants, little shiny black elephants, like the ebony elephants that stood on my grandmother's piano. I was sure of only one thing: I wanted to go with Arty and see it for myself as soon as I got better.

It was early August when I came downstairs again and about the middle of August before I could walk any distance. When I went out into the street everything seemed strange. I had not walked on the earth for eight weeks. Now, when I walked on it, it seemed to bounce under my feet. The things I had thought were ordinary seemed suddenly odd. The streets I had not seen for eight weeks seemed far stranger than the thought of the elephant's nest in a rhubarb tree.

One of the first things I did when I got downstairs was to go and see how far the Virginia creeper had gone. When I got round the street-corner I saw that someone had cut that part of it down. The little wine and green lizards had been slashed with a knife; they were withered by sun and the tendril-fingers were dead and fixed to the wall. As I looked at it I was not only hurt but I also knew that there was no longer any means of believing whether Arty had been right about it or wrong. I had to take his word again.

Then about three weeks later Arty and I set off one morning to find the elephant's nest in a rhubarb tree on his uncle's farm. Arty was about twelve years old, with big sloppy legs and thick golden hair all over his face, so that he looked almost, to me, like a grown man. All the time I had a feeling of being sorry for him, of knowing that he was simple, and yet of trusting him. I wanted too to make a discovery that I felt my father and mother and sister and perhaps other people had never made. I wanted to go home with a story of something impossible made possible.

It was very hot as we walked through the bare wheatfields out of the town. Heat danced like water on the distant edges of the white stubbles. We walked about a mile and then I asked Arty how much farther it was.

"Ain't much farther. Little way. Two three more fields. Little way, that's all."

I saw a farm in the near distance, against the woods. "Is that your uncle's farm?"

"Yeh," Arty said. "That's it. That's it."

"Where's the nest?" I said. "This side the farm or the other?"

"Other side," he said. "Just other side. Just little way other side, that's all."

We walked on for another half-hour and then when we reached the farm Arty said he'd made a mistake. His uncle's farm was the next farm. We walked on again and when we reached the next farm he said the same thing. Then the same thing again; then again. Finally I knew that it was time to turn back, that we were never going to see the thing we had come to see. As we walked back across the fields the heat of midday struck down on us as though it came through glass. Clear and direct and sickening on the sun-baked stubbles, it seemed to take away my strength and turn the tears of disappointment sour inside me.

When I got home I felt pale and weak and my feet were blistered and I felt like crying. Then when my mother asked me where I had been I said, "With Arty Whitehead, to find an elephant's nest in a rhubarb tree" they all burst out laughing. "Why, Arty isn't all there! That's all it is," they said, and I knew that they were right, and because I knew that they were right, and that what I had hoped to see never existed, I began crying at last.

Since that day, twenty-five years ago, a good deal has happened to me, but nothing at all has happened to Arty Whitehead. I no longer live in the same town; I have been across the world and I have grown up. But Arty still lives in the same town; he has never been anywhere and he has never grown up. And now he never will grow up. He is now a man of nearly forty but he is still the boy who ran after the bubble as big as a melon.

For the last twenty years Arty has worked for a baker. All he does is sit in the cart and hold the reins and tell the horse to stop and go. He does something that a boy of six could do. At the end of the week the baker gives him a shilling or two and every night he gives him a loaf of bread. Arty understands that. He understands the most fundamental thing about living: a loaf of bread. He understands perhaps all that anyone needs to understand.

Sometimes when I go back home I go to have my hair cut. Occasionally, as I sit in the barber's shop, Arty comes in. "Arty," the men say as they greet him, and I say "Arty," too, but Arty does not recognize me. I have grown up, whereas Arty's face is still the face of a boy. His eyes are still simple and remote and tender and as the men in the barber's shop talk Arty does not listen. He does not need to listen. They talk about Hitler, war in China, Mussolini, the cup-ties, the newspapers, women. Arty does not know who Hitler is; he does not know where China is or what is happening to China he does not know anything about women. He understands that he wants his hair cut. He understands a loaf of bread.

And there is also one other thing he understands. I sometimes see him walking out of the town. His glassy simple eyes are fixed on and perhaps beyond the distance. He does not walk very fast but he looks very happy. And because I know where he is going there is no doubt in my mind that he is very happy. He understands the most fundamental thing about living, a loaf of bread, and he also understands the most wonderful.

It seems to me that Arty understands what perhaps the rest of the world is trying to get at. He understands the elephant's nest in a rhubarb tree.

The Ox

THE Thurlows lived on a small hill. As though it were not high enough, the house was raised up, as on invisible stilts, with a wooden flight of steps to the front door. Exposed and isolated, the wind striking at it from all quarters, it seemed to have no part with the surrounding landscape. Empty ploughed lands, in winter-time, stretched away on all sides in wet steel curves.

At half-past seven every morning Mrs. Thurlow pushed her great rusty bicycle down the hill; at six every evening she pushed it back. Loaded, always, with grey bundles of washing, oilcans, sacks, cabbages, bundles of old newspaper, boughs of wind-blown wood, and bags of chicken food, the bicycle could never be ridden. It was a vehicle of necessity. Her relationship to it was that of a beast to a cart. Slopping along beside it, flat heavy feet pounding painfully along under mudstained skirts, her face and body ugly with lumpy angles of bone, she was like a beast of burden.

Coming out of the house, raised up even above the level of the small hill, she stepped into a country of wide horizons. This fact meant nothing to her. The world into which she moved was very small: from six to nine she cleaned for the two retired sisters, nine to twelve for the retired photographer, twelve-thirty to three for the poultry farm, four to six for the middle-aged bachelor. She did not think of going beyond the four lines which made up the square of her life. She thought of other people going beyond them, but this was different. Staring down at a succession of wet floors, working always for other people, against time, she had somehow got into the habit of not thinking about herself.

She thought much, in the same stolid pounding way as she pushed the bicycle, of other people: in particular of Thurlow, more particularly of her two sons. She had married late; the boys were nine and thirteen. She saw them realizing refined ambitions, making their way as assistants in shops, as clerks in offices, even as butlers. Heavily built, with faces having her own angular boniness, they moved with eyes on the ground. She had saved money for them. For fifteen years she had hoarded the scrubbing-and-washing money, keeping it in a bran bag under a mattress in the back bedroom. They did not know of it; she felt that no one, not even Thurlow, knew of it.

Thurlow had a silver plate in his head. In his own eyes it set him apart from other men. "I got a plate in me head. Solid silver. Enough silver to make a dozen spoons and a bit over. Solid. Beat that!" Wounded on the Marne, and now walking about with the silver plate in his head, Thurlow was a martyr. "I didn't ought to stoop. I didn't ought to do nothing. By rights. By rights I didn't ought to lift a finger." He was a hedge cutter. "Lucky I'm tall, else that job wouldn't be no good to me." He had bad days and good days, even days of genuine pain. "Me plate's hurting me! It's me plate. By God, it'll drive me so's I don't know what I'm doing! It's me plate again." And he would stand wild and vacant, rubbing his hands through his thin black hair, clawing his scalp as though to wrench out the plate and the pain.

Once a week, on Saturdays or Sundays, he came home a little tipsy, in a good mood, laughing to himself, riding his bicycle up the hill like some comic rider in a circus. "Eh? Too much be damned. I can ride me bike, can't I? S' long as I can ride me bike I'm all right." In the pubs he had only one theme, "I got a plate in me head. Solid silver," recited in a voice challenging the world to prove it otherwise.

All the time Mrs. Thurlow saved money. It was her creed. Sometimes people went away and there was no cleaning. She then made up the gap in her life by other work: picking potatoes, planting potatoes, dibbing cabbages, spudding roots, pea picking, more washing. In the fields she pinned up her skirt so that it stuck out behind her like a thick stiff tail, making her look like some bony ox. She did washing from five to six in the morning, and again from seven to nine in the evening. Taking in more washing, she tried to wash more quickly, against time. Somehow she succeeded, so that from nine to ten she had time for ironing. She worked by candlelight. Her movements were largely instinctive. She had washed and ironed for so long, in the same way, at the same time and place, that she could have worked in darkness.

There were some things, even, which could be done in darkness; and so at ten, with Thurlow and the sons in bed, she blew out the candle, broke up the fire, and sat folding the clothes or cleaning boots, and thinking. Her thoughts, like her work, went always along the same lines, towards the future, out into the resplendent avenues of ambitions, always for the two sons. There was a division in herself, the one part stolid and uncomplaining in perpetual labour, the other fretful and almost desperate in an anxiety to establish a world beyond her own. She had saved fifty-four pounds. She would make it a hundred. How it was to be done she could not think. The boys were growing, the cost of keeping them was growing. She trusted in some obscure providential power as tireless and indomitable as herself.

At eleven she went to bed, going up the wooden stairs in darkness, in her stockinged feet. She undressed in darkness, her clothes falling away to be replaced by a heavy grey nightgown that made her body seem still larger and more ponderous. She fell asleep almost at once, but throughout the night her mind, propelled by some inherent anxiety, seemed to work on. She dreamed she was pushing the bicycle down the hill, and then that she was pushing it up again; she dreamed she was scrubbing floors; she felt the hot stab of the iron on her spittled finger and then the frozen bite of icy swedes as she picked them off unthawed earth on bitter mornings. She counted her money, her mind going back over the years throughout which she had saved it, and then counted it again, in fear, to make sure, as though in terror that it might be gone in the morning.

★ ★ ★

294

She had one relaxation. On Sunday afternoons she sat in the kitchen alone, and read the newspapers. They were not the newspapers of the day, but of all the previous week and perhaps of the week before that. She had collected them from the houses where she scrubbed, bearing them home on the bicycle. Through them and by them she broke the boundaries of her world. She made excursions into the lives of other people: tragic lovers, cabinet ministers, Atlantic flyers, suicides, society beauties, murderers, kings. It was all very wonderful. But emotionally, as she read, her face showed no impression. It remained ox-like in its impassivity. It looked in some way indomitably strong, as though little things like beauties and suicides, murderers and kings, could have no possible effect on her. About three o'clock as she sat reading, Thurlow would come in, lumber upstairs, and sleep until about half-past four.

One Sunday he did not come in at three o'clock. It was after four when she heard the bicycle tinkle against the woodshed outside. She raised her head from the newspaper and listened for him to come in. Nothing happened. Then after about five minutes Thurlow came in, went upstairs, remained for some minutes, and then came down again. She heard him go out into the yard. There was a stir among the chickens as he lumbered about the woodshed.

Mrs. Thurlow got up and went outside, and there, at the door of the woodshed, Thurlow was just hiding something under his coat. She thought it seemed like his billhook. She was not sure. Something made her say:

"Your saw don't need sharpening again a'ready, does it?"

"That it does," he said. "That's just what it does. Joe Woods is going to sharp it." Thurlow looked upset and slightly wild, as he did when the plate in his head was hurting him. His eyes were a little drink-fired, dangerous. "I gonna take it down now, so's I can git it back to-night."

All the time she could see the saw itself hanging in the darkness of the woodshed behind him. She was certain then that he was lying, almost certain that it was the billhook he had under his coat.

She did not say anything else. Thurlow got on his bicycle and rode off, down the hill, his coat bunched up, the bicycle slightly crazy as he drove with one tipsy hand.

Something, as soon as he had gone, made her rush upstairs. She went into the back bedroom and flung the clothes off the mattress of the small iron bed that was never slept in. The money: it was all right. It was quite all right. She sat down heavily on the bed. And after a moment's anxiety her colour returned again — the solid, immeasurably passive calm with which she scrubbed, read the newspapers, and pushed the bicycle.

In the evening, the boys at church, she worked again. She darned socks, the cuffs of jackets, cleaned boots, sorted the washing for the following day. The boys must look well, respectable. Under the new scheme they went, now, to a secondary school in the town. She was proud of this, the first real stepping-stone to the higher things of the future. Outside, the night was windy, and she heard the now brief, now very prolonged moan of wind over the dark winter-ploughed land. She worked by candlelight. When the boys came in she lighted the lamp. In their hearts, having now some standard by which to judge her, they despised her a little. They hated the cheapness of the candlelight. When they had eaten and gone lumbering up to bed, like two colts, she blew out the lamp and worked by candlelight again. Thurlow had not come in.

He came in a little before ten. She was startled, not hearing the bicycle.

"You want something t' eat?"

"No," he said. He went straight into the scullery. She heard him washing his hands, swilling the sink, washing, swilling again.

"You want the light?" she called.

"No!"

He came into the kitchen. She saw his still-wet hands in the candlelight. He gave her one look and went upstairs without speaking. For some time she pondered on the memory of this look, not understanding it. She saw in it the wildness of the afternoon, as though the plate were hurting him, but now it had in addition fear, and, above fear, defiance.

She got the candle and went to the door. The wind tore the candle flame down to a minute blue bubble which broke, and she went across the yard, to the woodshed, in darkness. In the woodshed she put a match to the candle again, held the candle up at eye level, and looked at the walls. The saw hung on its nail, but there was no billhook. She made a circle with the candle, looking for the bicycle with dumb eyes. It was not there. She went into the house again. Candleless, very faintly perturbed, she went up to bed. She wanted to say something to Thurlow, but he was dead still, as though asleep, and she lay down herself, hearing nothing but the sound of Thurlow's breathing and, outside, the sound of the wind blowing across the bare land.

Asleep, she dreamed, as nearly always, about the bicycle, but this time it was Thurlow's bicycle and there was something strange about it. It had no handles, but only Thurlow's billhook where the handles should have been. She grasped the billhook, and in her dream she felt the pain of the blood rushing out of her hands, and she was terrified and woke up.

Immediately she put out her hands, to touch Thurlow. The bed was empty. That scared her. She got out of bed. "Thurlow! Bill! Thurlow! Thurlow!"

The wind had dropped, and it was quiet everywhere. She went downstairs. There, in the kitchen, she lighted the candle again and looked round. She tried the back door; it was unlocked and she opened it and looked out, feeling the small ground wind icy on her bare feet.

"Thurlow!" she said. "Bill! Thurlow!"

She could hear nothing, and after about a minute she went back upstairs. She looked in at the boys' bedroom. The boys were asleep, and the vast candle shadow of herself stood behind her and listened, as it were, while she listened. She went into her own bedroom: nothing. Thurlow was not there — nothing. Then she went into the back bedroom.

The mattress lay on the floor. And she knew, even before she began to look for it, that the money was gone. She knew that Thurlow had taken it.

Since there was nothing else she could

do, she went back to bed, not to sleep, but to lie there, oppressed but never in despondency, thinking. The money had gone, Thurlow had gone, but it would be all right. Just before five she got up, fired the copper, and began the washing. At seven she hung it out in long grey lines in the wintry grey light, holding the pegs like a bit in her teeth. A little after seven the boys came down, to wash in the scullery.

"Here, here! Mum! There's blood all over the sink!"

"Your dad killed a rabbit," she said. "That's all."

She lumbered out into the garden, to cut cabbages. She cut three large cabbages, put them in a sack, and, as though nothing had happened, began to prepare the bicycle for the day. She tied the cabbages on the carrier, two oilcans on the handlebars, and then on the crossbar a small bundle of washing, clean, which she had finished on Saturday. That was all: nothing much for a Monday.

At half-past seven the boys went across the fields, by footpath, to catch the bus for school. She locked the house, and then, huge, imperturbable, planting down great feet in the mud, she pushed the bicycle down the hill. She had not gone a hundred yards before, out of the hedge, two policemen stepped into the road to meet her.

"We was wondering if Mr. Thurlow was in?"

"No," she said, "he ain't in."

"You ain't seen him?"

"No, I ain't seen him."

"Since when?"

"Since last night."

"You mind," they said, "if we look round your place?"

"No," she said, "you go on up. I got to git down to Miss Hanley's." She began to push the bicycle forward, to go.

"No," they said. "You must come back with us."

So she turned the bicycle round and pushed it back up the hill again. "You could leave your bike," one of the policemen said. "No," she said, "I'd better bring it. You can never tell nowadays what folk are going to be up to."

Up at the house she stood impassively by while the two policemen searched the woodshed, the garden, and finally the house itself. Her expression did not change as they looked at the blood in the sink. "He washed his hands there last night," she said.

"Don't touch it," the policeman said. "Don't touch it." And then suspiciously, almost in implied accusation: "You ain't touched nothing — not since last night?"

"I got something else to do," she said.

"We'd like you to come along with us, Mrs. Thurlow," they said, "and answer a few questions."

"All right." She went outside and took hold of her bicycle.

"You can leave your bicycle."

"No," she said. "I'll take it. It's no naughty way, up here, from that village."

"We got a car down the road. You don't want a bike."

"I better take it," she said.

She wheeled the bicycle down the hill. When one policeman had gone in the car she walked on with the other. Ponderous, flat-footed, unhurried, she looked as though she could have gone on pushing the bicycle in the same direction, at the same pace, for ever.

They kept her four hours at the station. She told them about the billhook, the blood, the way Thurlow had come home and gone again, her waking in the night, Thurlow not being there, the money not being there.

"The money. How much was there?"

"Fifty-four pounds, sixteen and four-pence. And twenty-eight of that in sovereigns."

In return they told her something else.

"You know that Thurlow was in the Black Horse from eleven to two yesterday?"

"Yes, I dare say that's where he'd be. That's where he always is, Sundays."

"He was in the Black Horse, and for about two hours he was arguing with a man stopping down here from London. Arguing about that plate in his head. The man said he knew the plate was aluminium and Thurlow said he knew it was silver. Thurlow got very threatening. Did you know that?"

"No. But that's just like him."

"This man hasn't been seen since, and Thurlow hasn't been seen since. Except by you last night."

"Do you want me any more?" she said. "I ought to have been at Miss Hanley's hours ago."

"You realize this is very important, very serious?"

"I know. But how am I going to get Miss Hanley in, and Mrs. Acott, and then the poultry farm and then Mr. George?"

"We'll telephone Miss Hanley and tell her you can't go."

"The money," she said. "That's what I can't understand. The money."

* * *

It was the money which brought her, without showing it, to the edge of distress. She thought of it all day. She thought of it as hard cash, coin, gold and silver, hard-earned and hard-saved. But it was also something much more. It symbolized the future, another life, two lives. It was the future itself. If, as seemed possible, something terrible had happened and a life had been destroyed, it did not seem to her more terrible than the fact that the money had gone and that the future had been destroyed.

As she scrubbed the floors at the poultry farm in the late afternoon, the police telephoned for her again. "We can send the car for her," they said.

"I got my bike," she said. "I'll walk."

With the oilcans filled, and cabbages and clean washing now replaced by newspapers and dirty washing, she went back to the police station. She wheeled her bicycle into the lobby and they then told her how, that afternoon, the body of the man from London had been found, in a spinney, killed by blows from some sharp instrument like an axe. "We have issued a warrant for Thurlow's arrest," they said.

"You never found the money?" she said.

"No," they said. "No doubt that'll come all right when we find Thurlow."

That evening, when she got home, she fully expected Thurlow to be there, as

306

usual, splitting kindling wood with the billhook, in the outhouse, by candlelight. The same refusal to believe that life could change made her go upstairs to look for the money. The absence of both Thurlow and the money moved her to no sign of emotion. But she was moved to a decision.

She got out her bicycle and walked four miles, into the next village, to see her brother. Though she did not ride the bicycle, it seemed to her as essential as ever that she should take it with her. Grasping its handles, she felt a sense of security and fortitude. The notion of walking without it, helplessly, in the darkness, was unthinkable.

Her brother was a master carpenter, a chapel-going man of straight-grained thinking and purpose, who had no patience with slovenliness. He lived with his wife and his mother in a white-painted electrically lighted house whose floors were covered with scrubbed coco-matting. His mother was a small woman with shrill eyes and ironed-out mouth who could not hear well.

Mrs. Thurlow knocked on the door of

the house as though these people, her mother and brother, were strangers to her. Her brother came to the door and she said:

"It's Lil. I come to see if you'd seen anything o' Thurlow?"

"No, we ain't seen him. Summat up?"

"Who is it?" the old woman called.

"It's Lil," the brother said, in a louder voice. "She says have we seen anything o' Thurlow?"

"No, an' don't want!"

Mrs. Thurlow went in. For fifteen years her family had openly disapproved of Thurlow. She sat down on the edge of the chair nearest the door. Her large lace-up boots made large black mud prints on the virgin coco-matting. She saw her sister-in-law look first at her boots and then at her hat. She had worn the same boots and the same hat for longer than she herself could remember. But her sister-in-law remembered.

She sat untroubled, her eyes sullen, as though not fully conscious in the bright electric light. The light showed up the mud on her skirt, her straggling grey hair under the shapeless hat, the edges of her black coat weather-faded to a purplish grey.

"So you ain't heard nothing about Thurlow?" she said.

"No," her brother said. "Be funny if we had, wouldn't it? He ain't set foot in this house since Dad died." He looked at her hard. "Why? What's up?"

She raised her eyes to him. Then she lowered them again. It was almost a minute before she spoke.

"Ain't you heard?" she said. "They reckon he's done a murder."

"What's she say?" the old lady said. "I never heard her."

Mrs. Thurlow looked dully at her boots, at the surrounding expanse of coco-matting. For some reason the fissured pattern of the coco-matting, so clean and regular, fascinated her. She said: "He took all the money. He took it all and they can't find him."

"Eh? What's she say? What's she mumbling about?"

The brother, his face white, went over to the old woman. He said into her ear: "One of the boys is won a scholarship. She come over to tell us."

"Want summat to do, I should think, don't she? Traipsing over here to tell us that."

The man sat down at the table. He was very white, his hands shaking. His wife sat with the same dumb, shaking expression of shock. Mrs. Thurlow raised her eyes from the floor. It was as though she had placed on them the onus of some terrible responsibility.

"For God's sake," the man said, "when did it happen?"

All Mrs. Thurlow could think of was the money. "Over fifty pounds. I got it hid under the mattress. I don't know how he could have found out about it. I don't know. I can't think. It's all I got. I got it for the boys." She paused, pursing her lips together, squeezing back emotion. "It's about the boys I come."

"The boys?" The brother looked up, scared afresh. "He ain't — they — "

"I didn't know whether you'd have them here," she said. "Till it's blowed over. Till they find Thurlow. Till things are straightened out."

"Then they ain't found him?"

"No. He's done a bunk. They say as

310

soon as they find him I shall git the money."

"Yes," the brother said. "We'll have them here."

She stayed a little longer, telling the story dully, flatly, to the two scared pairs of eyes across the table and to the old shrill eyes, enraged because they could not understand, regarding her from the fireplace. An hour after she had arrived, she got up to go. Her brother said: "Let me run you back in the car. I got a car now. Had it three or four months. I'll run you back."

"No, I got my bike," she said.

She pushed the bicycle home in the darkness. At home, in the kitchen, the two boys were making a rabbit hutch. She saw that they had something of her brother's zeal for handling wood. She saw that their going to him would be a good thing. He was a man who had got on in the world: she judged him by the car, the white-painted house, the electric light, the spotless coco-matting. She saw the boys, with deep but inexpressible pride, going to the same height, beyond it.

"Dad ain't been home," they said.

She told them there had been a little trouble. "They think your dad took some money." She explained how it would be better for them, and for her, if they went to stay with her brother. "Git to bed now and I'll get your things packed."

"You mean we gotta go and live there?"

"For a bit," she said.

They were excited. "We could plane the wood for the rabbit hutch!" they said. "Make a proper job of it."

* * *

That night, and again on the following morning, she looked under the mattress for the money. In the morning the boys departed. She was slightly depressed, slightly relieved by their excitement. When they had gone she bundled the day's washing together and tied it on the bicycle. She noticed, then, that the back tyre had a slow puncture, that it was already almost flat. This worried her. She pumped up the tyre and felt a little more confident.

Then, as she prepared to push the

bicycle down the hill, she saw the police car coming along the road at the bottom. Two policemen hurried up the track to meet her.

"We got Thurlow," they said. "We'd like you to come to the station."

"Is he got the money?" she said.

"There hasn't been time," they said, "to go into that."

As on the previous morning she pushed her bicycle to the village, walking with one policeman while the other drove on in the car. Of Thurlow she said very little. Now and then she stopped and stooped to pinch the back tyre of the bicycle. "Like I thought. I got a slow puncture," she would say. "Yes, it's gone down since I blowed it up. I s'll have to leave it at the bike shop as we go by."

Once she asked the policeman if he thought that Thurlow had the money. He said, "I'm afraid he's done something more serious than taking money."

She pondered over this statement with dull astonishment. More serious? She knew that nothing could be more serious. To her the money was like a huge and irreplacable section of her life. It was part of herself, bone and flesh, blood and sweat. Nothing could replace it. Nothing, she knew with absolute finality, could mean so much.

In the village she left the bicycle at the cycle shop. Walking on without it, she lumbered dully from side to side, huge and unsteady, as though lost. From the cycle-shop window the repairer squinted after her, excited. Other people looked from other windows as she lumbered past, always a pace or two behind the policeman, her ill-shaped feet painfully set down. At the entrance to the police station there was a small crowd. She went heavily into the station. Policemen were standing about in a room. An inspector, many papers in his hand, spoke to her. She listened heavily. She looked about for a sign of Thurlow. The inspector said, with kindness, "Your husband is not here." She felt a sense of having been cheated. "They are detaining him at Metford. We are going over there now."

"You know anything about the money?" she said.

Five minutes later she drove away, with

the inspector and two other policemen, in a large black car. Travelling fast, she felt herself hurled, as it were, beyond herself. Mind and body seemed separated, her thoughts nullified. As the car entered the town, slowing down, she looked out of the side windows, saw posters: 'Metford Murder Arrest'. People, seeing policemen in the car, gaped. 'Murder Sensation Man Detained.'

Her mind registered impressions gravely and confusedly. People and posters were swept away from her and she was conscious of their being replaced by other people, the police station, corridors in the station, walls of brown glazed brick, fresh faces, a room, desks covered with many papers, eyes looking at her, box files in white rows appearing also to look at her, voices talking to her, an arm touching her, a voice asking her to sit down.

"I have to tell you, Mrs. Thurlow, that we have detained your husband on a charge of murder."

"He say anything about the money?"

"He has made a statement. In a few minutes he will be charged and then probably remanded for further inquiries.

You are at liberty to see him for a few moments if you would like to do so."

In a few moments she was standing in a cell, looking at Thurlow. He looked at her as though he did not know what had happened. His eyes were lumps of impressionless glass. He stood with long arms loose at his sides. For some reason he looked strange, foreign, not himself. It was more than a minute before she realized why this was. Then she saw that he was wearing a new suit. It was a grey suit, thick, ready-made, and the sleeves were too short for him. They hung several inches above his thick protuberant wrist bones, giving his hands a look of inert defeat.

"You got the money, ain't you?" she said. "You got it?"

He looked at her. "Money?"

"The money you took. The money under the mattress."

He stared at her. Money? He looked at her with a faint expression of appeal. Money. He continued to stare at her with complete blankness. Money?

"You remember," she said. "The money under the mattress."

"Eh?"

"The money. That money. Don't you remember?"

He shook his head.

After some moments she went out of the cell. She carried out with her the sense of Thurlow's defeat as she saw it expressed in the inert hands, the dead, stupefied face, and his vacant inability to remember anything. She heard the court proceedings without interest or emotion. She was oppressed by a sense of increasing bewilderment, a feeling that she was lost. She was stormed by impressions she did not understand. "I do not propose to put in a statement at this juncture. I ask for a remand until the sixteenth." "Remand granted. Clear the court."

This effect of being stormed by impressions continued outside the court, as she drove away again in the car. People. Many faces. Cameras. More faces. Posters. The old sensation of mind severed from body, of thoughts nullified. In the village, when the car stopped, there were more impressions: more voices, more people, a feeling of suppressed excitement. "We will run you home," the policemen said.

"No," she said. "I got my cleaning to do. I got to pick up my bicycle."

She fetched the bicycle and wheeled it slowly through the village. People looked at her, seemed surprised to see her in broad daylight, made gestures as though they wished to speak, and then went on. Grasping the handles of the bicycle, she felt a return of security, almost of comfort. The familiar smooth handlebars hard against her hands had the living response of other hands. They brought back her sense of reality: Miss Hanley, the cleaning, the poultry farm, the time she had lost, the boys, the money, the fact that something terrible had happened, the monumental fact of Thurlow's face, inert and dead, with its lost sense of remembrance.

Oppressed by a sense of duty, she did her cleaning as though nothing had happened. People were very kind to her. Miss Hanley made tea, the retired photographer would have run her home in his car. She was met everywhere by tender, remote words of comfort.

She pushed home her bicycle in the darkness. At Miss Hanley's, at the poultry farm, at the various places where she worked, the thought of the money had been partially set aside. Now, alone again, she felt the force of its importance more strongly, with the beginnings of bitterness. In the empty house she worked for several hours by candlelight, washing, folding, ironing. About the house the vague noises of wind periodically resolved themselves into what she believed for a moment were the voices of the two boys. She thought of the boys with calm unhappiness, and the thought of them brought back with renewed force the thought of the money. This thought hung over her with the huge preponderance of her own shadow projected on the ceiling above her.

On the following Sunday afternoon she sat in the empty kitchen, as usual, and read the stale newspapers. But now they recorded, not the unreal lives of other people, but the life of Thurlow and herself. She saw Thurlow's photograph. She read the same story told in different words in different papers. In all the stories there was an absence of all mention of the only thing that mattered. There was no single word about the money.

During the next few weeks much happened, but she did not lose the belief that the money was coming back to her. Nothing could touch the hard central core of her optimism. She saw the slow evolution of circumstances about Thurlow as things of subsidiary importance, the loss of the life he had taken and the loss of his own life as things which, terrible in themselves, seemed less terrible than the loss of ideals built up by her sweat and blood.

She knew, gradually, that Thurlow was doomed, that it was all over. She did not know what to do. Her terror seemed remote, muffled, in some way incoherent. She pushed the bicycle back and forth each day in the same ponderous manner as ever, her heavy feet slopping dully beside it.

When she saw Thurlow for the last time his face had not changed, one way or the other, from its fixed expression of defeat. Defeat was cemented into it with imperishable finality. She asked him about the money for the last time.

"Eh?"

"The money. You took it. What you do with it? That money. Under the mattress." For the first time she showed some sign of desperation. "Please, what you done with it? That money. My money?"

"Eh?" And she knew that he could not remember.

★ ★ ★

A day later it was all over. Two days later she pushed the bicycle the four miles to the next village, to see her brother. It was springtime, time for the boys to come back to her. Pushing the bicycle in the twilight, she felt she was pushing forward into the future. She had some dim idea, heavily dulled by the sense of Thurlow's death, that the loss of the money was not now so great. Money is money; death is death; the living are the living. The living were the future. The thought of the boys' return filled her with hopes for the future, unelated hopes, but quite real, strong enough to surmount the loss of both Thurlow and money.

At her brother's they had nothing to say. They sat, the brother, the mother, and the sister-in-law, and looked at her with eyes over which, as it were, the blinds had been drawn.

"The boys here?" she said.

"They're in the workshop," her brother said. "They're making a bit of a wheelbarrow."

"They all right?"

"Yes." He wetted his lips. His clean-planned mind had been scarred by events as though by a mishandled tool. "They don't know nothing. We kept it from 'em. They ain't been to school and they ain't seen no papers. They think he's in jail for stealing money."

She looked at him, dully. "Stealing money? That's what he did do. That money I told you about. That money I had under the mattress."

"Well," he said slowly, "it's done now."

"What did he do with it?" she said. "What d'ye reckon he done with it?"

He looked at her quickly, unable suddenly to restrain his anger. "Done with it? What d'ye suppose he done with it? Spent it. Threw it away. Boozed it. What else? You know what he was like. You knew! You had your eyes open. You knew what — "

"Will, Will," his wife said.

He was silent. The old lady said: "Eh? What's that? What's the matter now?"

The brother said, in a loud voice, "Nothing." Then more softly: "She don't know everything."

"I came to take the boys back," Mrs. Thurlow said.

He was silent again. He wetted his lips. He struck a match on the warm fire-hob. It spurted into a sudden explosion, igniting of its own volition. He seemed startled. He put the match to his pipe, let it go out.

He looked at Mrs. Thurlow, the dead match in his hands. "The boys ain't coming back no more," he said.

"Eh?" she said. She was stunned. "They ain't what?"

"They don't want to come back," he said.

She did not understand. She could not speak. Very slowly he said:

"It's natural they don't want to come

back. I know it's hard. But it's natural. They're getting on well here. They want to stop here. They're good boys. I could take 'em into the business."

She heard him go on without hearing the individual words. He broke off, his face relieved — like a man who has liquidated some awful obligation.

"They're my boys," she said. "They got a right to say what they shall do and what they shan't do."

She spoke heavily, without bitterness.

"I know that," he said. "That's right. They got a right to speak. You want to hear what they got to say?"

"Yes, I want to," she said.

Her sister-in-law went out into the yard at the back of the house. Soon voices drew nearer out of the darkness and the two boys came in.

"Hullo," she said.

"Hello, Mum," they said.

"Your Mum's come," the carpenter said, "to see if you want to go back with her."

The two boys stood silent, awkward, eyes glancing past her.

"You want to go?" the carpenter said.

"Or do you want to stay here?"

"Here," the elder boy said. "We want to stop here."

"You're sure o' that?"

"Yes," the other said.

Mrs. Thurlow stood silent. She could think of nothing to say in protest or argument or persuasion. Nothing she could say would, she felt, give expression to the inner part of herself, the crushed core of optimism and faith.

She stood at the door, looking back at the boys. "You made up your minds, then?" she said. They did not speak.

"I'll run you home," her brother said.

"No," she said. "I got my bike."

She went out of the house and began to push the bicycle slowly home in the darkness. She walked with head down, lumbering painfully, as though direction did not matter. Whereas, coming, she had seemed to be pushing forward into the future, she now felt as if she were pushing forward into nowhere.

After a mile or so she heard a faint hissing from the back tyre. She stopped, pressing the tyre with her hand. "It's slow," she thought; "it'll last me." She pushed forward. A little later it seemed to her that the hissing got worse. She stopped again, and again felt the tyre with her hand. It was softer now, almost flat.

She unscrewed the pump and put a little air in the tyre and went on. "I better stop at the shop," she thought, "and have it done."

In the village the cycle shop was already in darkness. She pushed past it. As she came to the hill leading up to the house she lifted her head a little. It seemed to her suddenly that the house, outlined darkly above the dark hill, was a long way off. She had for one moment an impression that she would never reach it.

She struggled up the hill. The mud of the track seemed to suck at her great boots and hold her down. The wheels of the bicycle seemed as if they would not turn, and she could hear the noise of the air dying once again in the tyre.

1	31	61	91	121	151	181	211	241	271	301	331
2	32	62	92	122	152	182	212	242	272	302	332
3	33	63	93	123	153	183	213	243	273	303	333
4	34	64	94	124	154	184	214	244	274	304	334
5	35	65	95	125	155	185	215	245	275	305	335
6	36	66	96	126	156	186	216	245	276	306	336
7	37	67	97	127	157	187	217	247	277	307	337
8	38	68	98	128	158	188	218	248	278	308	338
9	39	69	99	129	159	189	219	249	279	309	339
10	40	70	100	130	160	190	220	250	280	310	340
11	41	71	101	131	161	191	221	251	281	311	341
12	42	72	102	132	162	192	222	252	282	312	342
13	43	73	103	133	163	193	223	253	283	313	343
14	44	74	104	134	164	194	224	254	284	314	344
15	45	75	105	135	165	195	225	255	285	315	345
16	46	76	106	136	166	196	226	256	286	316	346
17	47	77	107	137	167	197	227	257	287	317	347
18	48	78	108	138	168	198	228	258	288	318	348
19	49	79	109	139	169	199	229	259	289	319	349
20	50	80	110	140	170	200	230	260	290	320	350
21	51	81	111	141	171	201	231	261	291	321	351
22	52	82	112	142	172	202	232	262	292	322	352
23	53	83	113	143	173	203	233	263	293	323	353
24	54	84	114	144	174	204	234	264	294	324	354
25	55	85	115	145	175	205	235	265	295	325	355
26	56	86	116	146	176	206	236	266	296	326	356
27	57	87	117	147	177	207	237	267	297	327	357
28	58	88	118	148	178	208	238	268	298	328	358
29	59	89	119	149	179	209	239	269	299	329	359
30	60	90	120	150	180	210	240	270	300	330	360